DANGEROUS SUMMER

Anya has been in love with Zack Anderson, her brother-in-law, from childhood. Since her sister's tragic death a year ago, Anya has only his secretary as a rival for his affections — and tensions mount when they stay together at Zack's villa in the south of France. But then the summer erupts into violence, and life at the Villa Donmarie becomes a nightmare when Anya realises someone she knows might be a double murderer. It might even be someone she loves . . .

BRENDA CASTLE

DANGEROUS SUMMER

Complete and Unabridged

LINFORD
Leicester

First published in Great Britain in 1975

First Linford Edition
published 2014
by arrangement with
Robert Hale Limited
London

A catalogue record for this book is available
from the British Library.

ISBN 978–1–4448–1934–2

Published by
F. A. Thorpe (Publishing)
Anstey, Leicestershire

Set by Words & Graphics Ltd.
Anstey, Leicestershire
Printed and bound in Great Britain by
T. J. International Ltd., Padstow, Cornwall

This book is printed on acid-free paper

In ever loving memory of
my darling father,
Ben Appleson.
The kindest man and the best
friend anyone could
ever have, and the finest man
I have ever known.

1

The sky was reflected in the sea. It was the clear cloudless azure that has been eulogised by poets and singers since time began. But the girl who came rushing out of the villa which stood on the top of the cliff had no interest in the beauty around her. Clad only in a pair of brief shorts and a tee shirt she ran along the edge of the swimming pool, watched by several pairs of curious eyes. For once she ignored a cry for attention from the little boy who was paddling at the shallow end; she ran on, towards the low wall which edged the cliff, where the children were forbidden to go. Below the cliff the Mediterranean creamed gently against the tiny strip of sand which was practically inaccessible to anyone other than the inhabitants of the villa; a thick pine wood screened it from the nearby village of St. Brilac and its seasonal invasion of visitors.

The girl paused at the top of the steps that had been hewn in the red porphyry of the cliff. She caught her breath and glanced back, saw a figure emerge from the villa, and began to run down the narrow, sometimes treacherous, steps. If she should fall, not only was it a long way down, but the base of the cliff was peppered with jutting rocks, as sharp as shark's teeth. Halfway down she paused again, partly to catch her breath and partly to see if she were being pursued. The villa stood, stark white, against the dramatic background of the Esterel.

Of course no one came. She hadn't thought he would. He would shrug it off, amused at her reaction. Zack would not trouble to pursue her to the beach. She knew him well enough to be aware of that.

She walked down the rest of the steps. Stunted olive trees, cacti and aloes clung desperately to the face of the cliff. A renegade branch whipped against her face but she hardly noticed the discomfort. When she reached the beach, which was but a few yards wide, she removed her thonged sandals and allowed her feet to sink into the warm damp sand. She glanced upwards automatically but now the villa was out of sight all she could see was the dark wall of cliff soaring upwards.

The girl sat down on a flat-topped rock and stared out to sea, her chin propped on her hands and her elbows supported by her knees. The sea glistened like crystal in the harsh sunlight of late afternoon. On the horizon were several sailing craft, probably bound for Cannes, Nice, Villefranche or Monte Carlo. They were all unrecognisable but the girl knew they would all be sleek and shiny craft, made from polished mahogany and brass.

She drew a sigh. What a fool she had been to react in that way just because Zack had kissed her. How he would be laughing at her now, for running away, to have revealed her feelings for him so patently.

She closed her eyes and relived that kiss. It had been harsh and searching, the realisation of a thousand sensual dreams. What did she feel now it had happened at last? Ecstacy and triumph? Just plain panic.

Her eyes opened wide again. It was too soon to go back. The sea sparkled. It was too inviting. She slid off the rock and in seconds had stripped off the tee shirt and the shorts and was running joyously into the sea.

The water was delightfully cold after the heat of the day. It brought her to reason at last. The shock was over. Now she could return to the Villa Donmarie with some degree of serenity. Zack's love was all she had ever wanted since she was thirteen years old. No need to let Marika's ghost come between them. Marika was dead. It was a fact — heartbreaking, but a fact nevertheless, and now Zack was free, free to love again.

4

Her feet touched sand and she waded back to the beach with water dripping from her head to her feet, plastering her hair in a cap around her head. Her feet were still in the water when she stopped, momentarily distracted from her thoughts. Then she stiffened, first with fear and then with anger.

The sun had reflected off some metal or glass object and it took only seconds for the girl to realise someone was watching her through field glasses. Someone who must be standing at the edge of the pine woods.

From frozen immobility she moved with a speed of which she believed she was incapable. She snatched up her clothes and her hands trembled in her haste to pull up the shorts and throw the tee shirt over her head. She had only just pulled it down when someone emerged from the dense interior of the wood and began to pick his way with sure-footed ease across the foam washed rocks leading to the little beach.

A very short time ago she had run

from the villa; now it was a haven for which she longed. Her heart was beating so fast she thought it might burst as she began to back away.

'Hey!' the man shouted as he approached across the sands. 'What do you think you're doing?'

The girl stopped retreating towards the steps. She was still trembling, but now it was with anger not fear.

'Wh . . . what do you mean?' she stammered in halting French. 'How dare you spy on me?'

The man looked less angry, more uncertain. He was swinging a pair of field glasses in his hand; now he tightened the strap around his wrist. 'Are you English?'

'Yes.'

He flung one hand in the air. 'Then what the hell are you doing bathing . . . *naked* where anyone can see you.'

The girl felt the colour flowing into her cheeks. His English was as good as his French. 'You were spying on me,' she repeated.

'I certainly was not. I happen to like boats. I was watching *them*.' He looked disgusted and she felt ashamed. 'I didn't expect to see a . . . kid strip to the buff and wade into the sea.'

'A kid! Look here, Mr. who-ever-you-are, I am quite old enough to do as I wish. No one ever comes to this beach.'

'Until today,' he answered, still looking at her steadily. He watched her with a pair of steely grey eyes. His anger was real and she knew for certain he was no peeping-Tom. 'Haven't your parents more sense than to allow you out alone?'

'My parents are dead and I am old enough to be out alone!' She fumbled for words for a moment or two, feeling near to tears, and then she began to back away again. 'If you insist on going on at me in this way . . . I shall be forced to call the police.'

He stared hard at her for a moment or two and then began to scratch his head, ruffling, as he did so, his mop of unruly brown hair.

'You're not a kid, are you?'

The girl tossed back her head in a gesture of defiance. 'Certainly not.'

His own anger had gone. She couldn't understand why he'd been angry anyway.

'Look, I'm sorry I flew at you.' She said nothing. 'I know what you did is common enough along this coast; it just seemed a stupid thing to do while you're alone. It might have been someone . . . other than myself who happened along here.'

She scuffed her toe in the sand. 'It was a momentary impulse.' She looked up at him steadily. 'I don't think it will happen again.'

'I'm relieved to hear it.' He grinned for the first time and then considered her carefully. 'My name's . . . Nolan. Jared Nolan.'

'You're an American, aren't you? Your French is excellent, though. Mine is very elementary. I'm doing my best to improve it while I'm here . . . ' Her voice died away uncertainly.

'I'm Canadian; that accounts for it. At the moment I'm based at St. Brilac. I've chartered a small boat for a month and I'm trying to see as much of the area as I can in that time.'

She held out her hand shyly. 'I'm Anya Kovacks.'

At first he hesitated and then he took her hand briefly in his. 'I thought you said you were English.'

'British. Yes, I am.' She laughed and looked upwards. 'I'm staying at the Villa Donmarie for the summer. My brother-in-law owns it.'

He looked up too although there was nothing to be seen but a few stunted trees overhanging the cliff. 'I was curious about that villa. I thought it must belong to a millionaire or a film star. There are quite a few celebrities living around here. Is your brother-in-law one?'

'Not quite,' Anya answered, laughing again. 'He's Zack Anderson, the playwright. He's had quite a bit of success over the past few years.'

9

Jared Nolan nodded slowly. 'I have heard of him.'

He glanced at his watch and Anya was reminded that she was alone with a stranger. Instinctively she knew she had nothing to fear from this man, but still . . .

She began to back away again, smiling self-consciously as she did so. She had the feeling he could read her mind very easily.

'I must go. Everyone will wonder where I am.'

He nodded slowly again, as if deep in thought. 'I'm sorry I frightened you . . . '

'It's all right. I deserved it.'

She paused before beginning her careful negotiation of the steps. He was still standing where she had left him, his feet planted firmly in the sand. He raised his hand in salute and she waved back and smiled at him, still with some uncertainty.

When she paused again halfway up the cliff he was still there, still watching her, still frowning thoughtfully.

★ ★ ★

'I'm quite sure, when I saw you coming into the house, you were soaking wet from head to toe, Anya.'

She looked up sharply. Helen Anderson had come unheard into the salon. She always walked quietly and quickly, and managed to be everywhere at once, mostly where Anya didn't want her to be.

She wished she could like Zack's mother, but she couldn't. Mrs. Anderson had never been intentionally unkind but in her manner was a disapproval Anya could not ignore. Really, she knew, it stemmed from a disapproval of Zack's marriage to her sister, Marika, and now Marika was dead Anya was very much aware that Mrs. Anderson wished Zack would make a new start, a complete break.

'Yes,' she answered at last, putting aside the book she had been enjoying. 'I went down to the beach and decided to have a . . . swim.'

Helen Anderson's prim little face broke into a disbelieving smile. 'With your clothes on?'

Anya looked at her steadily, deciding that a lie would be preferable to the truth in this instance. 'Would you have preferred me to take them off?'

The large picture window looked out on an infinity of inky blackness which, a short time before, had been the sea and the sky. The perfumes of jasmin and roses mingled and floated through the partially open patio doors.

Mrs. Anderson laughed in embarrassment. 'Really, Anya, dear, for a girl of . . . you're twenty now, aren't you? . . . you're still extremely childish.'

'*In delay there lies no plenty;*
Then come kiss me, sweet and
twenty,
Youth's a stuff will not endure.'

Anya quoted Shakespeare's lines, flourishing her hands in a dramatic gesture. Mrs. Anderson didn't know whether to smile or not. She walked across to the window, her soft-soled shoes making no noise on the tiled floor.

'What was that you said, dear?' she asked, making a great pretence of nonchalance.

Anya was immediately regretful. She pitied Helen Anderson a little; an ordinary woman who had been swept from suburbia on the wave of her son's wealth and fame. It was often a struggle, Anya guessed, for her to keep afloat.

'It was Shakespeare — Twelfth Night. I played the part of Olivia in a school production once and I still remember every line of it.' She paused as the other woman struggled for something to say. Still repentant Anya went on, 'Your hair looks nice, Helen. Have you had it done today?'

The woman patted her blue rinsed hair and smiled genuinely now. 'There's a girl in St. Brilac who is an absolute artist. Apparently she has some very important clients who come all the way from Cap Ferrat and St. Tropez . . . '

Anya was already sorry she had mentioned the subject which was only brought to an end by a faltering step in the doorway. Both women turned. Anya stiffened slightly as Althea Kent came into the room. The presence of Zack's secretary always had an odd effect on Anya. Not only was this young woman extremely efficient at her work but she had looks and a dress sense that no good secretary had a right to possess — according to Anya, that is. Now Anya knew without doubt she was jealous that such an attractive female was so close to Zack. Had he kissed her too? she wondered as her gaze slid away from Althea's lightly rouged lips.

From her sharp, almost indiscernible, intake of breath Anya knew that Althea had a similar effect on Helen Anderson. Anya was forced to smile to herself; the cause of the dislike was a similar one, only Helen was bound to dislike any woman who came close to Zack; even the woman he had married.

'Good evening, Mrs. Anderson — Anya,' said Althea in the detached, almost icy manner which was characteristic of her. She never seemed to display an iota of emotion. To everyone she was the perfect secretary, cool and detached, but her eyes betrayed her to Anya . . . when they were looking at Zack.

The two women murmured a greeting and Althea sank down on to the end of the sofa with the full expanse of it between her and the other girl.

'Have you seen Zack tonight, Althea?'

Helen's tone was deceptively light. Anya knew it cost her dear to have to ask this girl about her son.

Althea raised her eyes. 'He's been struggling with one particular passage all day. You know how he refuses to leave anything until it's absolutely right. He's such a perfectionist.'

Helen came away from the window, wringing her hands together in anguish. 'He works too hard. There's no need . . .'

'Zack finds the need,' said Anya quickly. 'He needs to create. It's his instinct.'

'Well said, Anya!'

She looked around sharply and her face suffused with colour as Zack came into the room. His shoes made no sound on the floor either. Like his mother, surprisingly for a man, he walked with a very light step.

Helen rushed up to him and he put his arm around her shoulders and kissed her lightly on her well-powdered cheek.

'Mother has no objection to living off the fruits of my endeavours, have you, my love?'

'Really, Zack, you know I only care for your health and well-being.'

His hand slipped from her shoulders. 'Drinks everyone?' He didn't wait for a reply before starting to mix, with an expert hand, his own personal cocktail named after his first successful play. After years of holding down dead-end jobs, writing in his spare time, success came sweet to Zack Anderson.

Althea automatically went to join him at the drinks trolley, handing out the foaming, iced liquid which Zack poured from a silver cocktail shaker. Helen watched them with scarcely concealed resentment whilst Anya watched them with interest. They were well-matched, both of medium height, one dark and one fair, both looking like a magazine version of the perfect couple.

Zack brought Anya's drink himself. He knew she disliked his 'Happy People' cocktail. It was the first time they had met face to face since that kiss earlier in the afternoon. His lips curved into a smile as she took the glass and their hands touched in spite of her attempt to avoid any contact with him.

'A sweet sherry for sweet Anya.'

Her eyes met his and she felt the now familiar tremor run through her veins. Then Althea said, 'Cèlie was reading the children a story when I came past the nursery. She was reading it in French.'

Zack moved away. Anya breathed at last. 'It's good for them to learn French while they're young enough to absorb it naturally,' he said. 'They won't have any difficulty conjugating French verbs when the time comes for them to go to school.'

'Soon they'll forget they can speak English,' commented his mother.

'We'll try to find an English nanny when Cèlie leaves us in the autumn.'

He was looking at Anya again but she said nothing and he looked away again. 'It's not a very easy task these days, I'm afraid,' he murmured.

'But we must try,' his mother insisted. 'These foreign girls are all very well but your children, Zack — my grandchildren — are English.'

Zack smiled across at Anya and Althea said pointedly, 'A nanny is, after all, a short-term answer. Marika looked after the children herself with only the ordinary domestic help.'

No one said anything for a moment or two and then Zack said to Anya, gazing over the rim of his glass, 'You've changed in this last year, Anya.' She became alert. 'Last year you were a charming child. Now you're . . . different. Your hair suits you cut short.'

'Yes, doesn't it?' cut in Helen. To Anya her tone was too bright, not quite sincere.

She ran one hand through her dark blonde locks. 'It seemed the only thing to do at the time. It was always falling down. I think the problem is that it's too heavy.'

'I have no trouble with mine.'

Anya looked at Althea. Every silver hair was carefully in its place. It would be difficult to imagine her hair falling from its pins in disarray, tumbling to her shoulders, being caressed by Zack's fingers . . .

She looked away quickly. 'As I said, mine is too heavy to stay neatly pinned,' she murmured.

She looked at Zack again. Against the white of his dinner jacket he looked darker than usual. His eyes were

19

fathomless, his hair sleek, his cheek smooth. Anya suddenly remembered the man she had met on the beach. How different he was. Unshaven as Zack never was, with a mop of unruly brown hair that looked as if it had never seen a comb. She couldn't imagine Jared Nolan wearing anything other than an open-necked shirt and a pair of faded denims. She couldn't imagine Zack looking anything other than he did now — the realisation of all she wanted in a man. All she had ever wanted.

'I met a man on the beach today,' she said suddenly.

Zack's lips curved into an amused smile. Anya didn't know what reaction she had expected from him, only it wasn't this.

'A man? Good heavens!' murmured his mother, and Anya wondered what her reaction would have been if she said she had seen a Martian. 'I thought our little beach was secluded from the tourist invasion.'

'You talk like a native, Mother,' her son said, his indulgence spiked a little with acid.

'You shouldn't talk to strangers,' added Helen.

'I could hardly ignore him.'

Zack put down his glass. 'I rather suspect he was young.'

Anya shrugged slightly, wishing she hadn't mentioned her meeting with Jared Nolan. 'Fairly. He's got a boat, moored at St. Brilac.'

'Handsome?' asked Zack, smiling mischievously.

Anya pretended to consider, determined not to be disconcerted by his teasing. 'Pleasant rather than handsome, I should say.'

'You'd best be careful,' Althea said, laughing, 'these Frenchmen can be very charming. They can seduce a woman before she knows what has happened to her.'

'*I* wouldn't know about that,' Anya answered, smiling stiffly. 'Anyway, this man's a Canadian.'

'Canadian?' echoed Zack. He looked mildly interested now. 'Which part of Canada?'

'How should I know?' Anya was irritated. They were all treating her like an adolescent in the throes of a first infatuation. She didn't want to speak about it any more. She'd been a fool to mention it.

'I'm sure he gave you his name.'

Zack was looking at her keenly. A shiver of excitement ran up her spine. He was jealous! How marvellous!

'Jared Nolan.'

Zack continued to look at her steadily for a moment or two. Anya stared back boldly.

'I prefer bathing in the pool,' said Althea, smiling sweetly.

'Althea is right,' added Helen, 'the pool is perfectly adequate for swimming, and much safer if any problems do crop up . . . '

Her voice died away. Everyone present knew what she was referring to.

'I prefer the sea,' Anya answered

quietly a moment later, still feeling slightly rebellious. They had succeeded in making her feel foolish, only she wasn't quite sure why. 'I don't like to feel like a goldfish in a bowl,' she added.

Zack, she was well aware, was still smiling indulgently, still looking at her.

Helen put down her glass. 'I think it's time we went in for dinner.'

She stood up and Anya felt suddenly bitter. How she enjoys being the mistress of Zack's house, she thought, now that Marika's dead. But Zack won't remain unmarried and if he wants me . . .

Althea followed Helen out of the salon. Anya would have followed but Zack sprang to his feet and put his hand on her arm to detain her.

'Mother's right, Anya, you shouldn't go there alone. There could be any number of unsavoury characters roaming the pine wood and the beach at this time of the year. The camping site is nothing more than a hippy commune these days.'

'It's always been perfectly safe.' She wondered what he would say if he knew she had been bathing naked. 'Are you concerned for me, Zack?' she asked softly, looking directly into his eyes which were very near to her.

'You know I am.' He hesitated, considering her carefully. 'I didn't mean to upset you this afternoon, Sweetie. I want you to understand that.'

'I do.' Her voice was no more than the tiniest of whispers.

He didn't relinquish his hold on her arm. 'This year's been hell for me. Since Marika died I've not looked at a woman; I've not even been able to write up until these past two months ... I meant it when I said you'd changed ... '

Anya could look at him no longer. 'I know how difficult things have been for you, Zack. She was my sister.'

'Perhaps that's why I'm so drawn to you. I am, Anya, and that's the truth of it.'

Her heart beat unevenly. She felt

triumphant, but at the same time afraid. After seven years of silent worship and hopeless adoration it was all too sudden.

'You'll have to give me time, Zack. For a great deal of my life I've thought of you as a brother. Anything else will take some adjusting to.'

'But you will,' he insisted, 'you will come to look on me as something more than your brother-in-law.'

He was not asking a question, for he already knew the answer. He had pulled her even closer; his lips were near to her ear. Not far away Helen could be heard telling them not to dawdle. She couldn't imagine how Marika had endured her mother-in-law's constant presence. Helen in her dislike of Marika hadn't realised how lucky she was to have been endured by her daughter-in-law. I wouldn't have her here permanently, she vowed.

'Anya!' Zack insisted.

She looked at him then and he drew her closer, kissing her gently on the lips.

'Well, Anya, do you think you could come to care for me?'

Helen's fractious voice was heard again, making Zack's beautiful kiss seem almost obscene.

'Where are those two, Althea? Do go and hurry them or the consommé will be cold.'

Anya pulled away from him as Althea's footsteps came inexorably closer.

'Yes, Zack. Oh, yes.'

2

Anya scrambled over the foam-washed rocks that separated the little beach from the edge of the pine wood. For those unwilling to get their feet wet there was no access from the wood to the beach and this was the factor that kept it isolated. Anyway, there was a much bigger and better beach at the other side of St. Brilac which most visitors preferred to use. Being the only member of the household willing to clamber over the rocks, Anya used the short-cut whenever she wanted to go to St. Brilac. The others made the slightly longer journey by way of the road that ran along the cliff top and swooped into the village.

The pine wood was only a small one, hardly a wood at all; it took only a minute or two to pass through it. As she walked Anya's footsteps were muted by a carpet of pine needles and, above her, birds swooped in the higher branches which, because of their density, almost hid the sky from view. It was dark in the wood even though it was still early afternoon and involuntarily Anya shuddered, which was odd, for she was not by nature timid or fanciful. The trouble with this place, she told herself, is that anyone could creep up unheard.

She paused at the sound of a noise nearby. A girl laughed. A man's voice answered. Anya hurried on. The wood was a popular meeting place for lovers, secluded and secretive. Lots of young people, from all over the world, met at the international camping site which bordered the road between the villa and the village. In fact the silence was incongruous, for the road could not be more than two hundred yards away, but the wide flanks of sea pines, growing close together, muffled the sound of traffic.

Anya drew a small sigh of relief when

the trees began to thin. She had gone through the wood time and time again without being troubled by the silence. Perhaps, she mused, it was the changing relationship with Zack that was changing *her*.

Anya hadn't seen him at all this morning. He had been hard at work since an early breakfast, writing in longhand whilst Althea's typewriter in the office beyond Zack's study had hardly stopped. Now he had the desire to write again he was working twice as hard as anyone should.

Anya spent the morning with the children, five-year-old Jason and two-year-old Penny, and now, after handing them back to Cèlie who had been employed to look after them for the summer she was free to visit St. Brilac. When she had left the villa Helen had been sitting in the shade and Anya knew she would not be missed by her. But she couldn't help but be troubled by thoughts of Zack and Althea closeted together so much. Working together promoted a particular kind of intimacy.

St. Brilac was once just a picturesque fishing village and typically poor. Now there were several cafés and bars, and two hotels on the beach at the far side of the village, and an annual influx of summer visitors. Anya walked slowly along the edge of the quay. The boats moored there were mainly small craft belonging to the local inhabitants and the mainly French tourists who came to St. Brilac. The fishermen's houses rose in tiers up the cliff and their white stonework and red tiled roofs stood out harshly against the dark red of the cliff itself. She drew in a deep breath of salty air. St. Brilac had remained relatively unspoiled, mainly because there was nowhere for the property speculators to build.

She walked across the quay to one of the bars which overlooked the busiest part of St. Brilac. Its tables spilled out into the street and most of them were occupied. Anya pushed her way through the crowd inside the bar, waving to the barman who smiled when he caught sight of her.

'*Bonjour*, Mademoiselle Anya,' he shouted above the buzz of conversation. 'The usual?'

She laughed, eyeing with relish the tempting array of cakes and fruit tarts on the counter. 'The usual, Jules. How is business today?'

'Good!'

Anya inhaled the unmistakable tang of French tobacco. When she was at home, in the Tube, or in a store somewhere, the smell of someone smoking a French cigarette always reminded her of this idyllic spot.

She reached out over someone's head for her iced Coke. She paid for the drink and threaded her way outside again. She found a vacant table and sank down into a chair, happy to be able to watch the world go by with no real demands on her time; happy to be here in France with Zack; happy that he was coming to look on her as a woman.

But she was sad too; sad because if Marika had lived she would have remained for ever his little sister.

A movement on one of the boats across the quay caught her attention. She lowered her sunglasses slowly over her nose as a man came out of the cabin and straightened up. Jared Nolan. She hadn't expected him to be here still. There was little to keep a visitor here for more than a day or two. She had been so sure he would have moved on by now. The sophistication of Cannes and Nice invariably beckoned.

He was wearing the same shirt and faded denims he had worn yesterday, but the shirt looked crisp and creased as if he'd washed it and hadn't quite known how to iron it. He stood on the deck of his hired boat and took some time to look around him. So far he hadn't seen her so she sank back in the chair and hoped he would pass by. As he jumped on to the quay, at the same time shouting a greeting to a man on the next boat, Anya pushed her sunglasses on again and continued to sip at her ice cold drink.

Jared Nolan came striding across the quay, apparently making straight for her and she caught her breath, but when he smiled and waved it was to a group of people who were sitting at a table nearby. She watched him covertly as he conversed easily in French with them for a few minutes. His back was towards her but he was near enough for her to reach out and touch if she wished to do so, which she did not.

After a moment or two she heard him decline an invitation to join his friends for a drink and as he bid them goodbye he turned round slowly and she knew he had been aware of her all the time.

'It's Miss Kovacks,' he said with an air of great surprise, 'and looking very charming too, although not quite so charming as the first time I set eyes on her.'

Anya was staring out to sea. She looked up with deliberate slowness, hoping that any heightening of her colour would be attributed to the effects of the sun. Slowly she removed her sunglasses and looked at him. His grey eyes were, to her chagrin, filled with malicious amusement.

'Mr. Nolan, isn't it?' she said coolly.

He wasn't deceived by her apparent detachment.

'So you *do* remember me?'

She gave him a tight little smile. 'Of course I do — on the beach yesterday.'

'That sounds as if, perhaps, you meet many men the same way.' Her lips tightened and he went on quickly, 'May I buy you a drink? Another . . . Coke perhaps.'

She shrugged. 'You may if you wish. A cassis this time, please.'

His eyes flickered momentarily and then he smiled as he went inside, leaving her vexed at the impulse that had made her accept his company. But she hardly had time to regret the impulse, for he had returned with her cassis and a dry vermouth for himself.

For several minutes nothing was said

between them. Jared Nolan seemed happy enough to gaze about him, waving from time to time to an acquaintance who was passing by.

Anya watched him from behind her sunglasses which she had put on again. They were a shield behind which she could hide, although she hated herself for feeling the need to hide away from this man. Again she compared him to Zack. If they stood side by side Jared Nolan would tower by inches above her brother-in-law; Zack and his aesthetic leanness, Jared Nolan and his craggy masculinity.

He turned and Anya knew he had been aware of her stealthy observation of him. He smiled and then raised his glass of vermouth.

'A votre santé!'

Anya did likewise, saying quickly, 'You mentioned, yesterday, having chartered your boat for the month. Do you intend to remain here all that time?'

He sipped at the vermouth appreciatively. Then he replaced the glass on the table and sitting back in his chair he gazed at her for a moment or two.

'I believe I will. I rather like the scenery around here.'

It took a considerable amount of will-power for Anya to resist the temptation to throw the cassis in his complacent face. He was apparently quite determined not to let her forget the circumstances of their first meeting, and equally determined to embarrass her about it as often as the opportunity arose.

Before she could find a suitably acid answer he asked, 'How long do *you* intend to stay?'

'I'm not sure. For the summer anyway.'

He whistled softly. 'No ties at home?' he asked in some surprise. 'Aren't you lucky?'

'That isn't the way I feel about it,' she murmured in reply.

She removed her sunglasses at last and laid them on the table in front of her.

'Green,' he said with an air of amazement. 'I *knew* they were green.'

She looked up at him. 'What are you talking about?'

'I thought your eyes were green but I wasn't sure. It could have been anger yesterday.'

'It might just be anger today, Mr. Nolan.'

He laughed. 'No, you're not angry with me. Not today.'

She picked up her bag and glasses without looking at him again. 'I must go, Mr. Nolan. Thank you for the drink.'

'You haven't finished it.'

'I've had enough.'

He reached out as she stood up and put his hand over hers. It was a strong hand, well-manicured but unlike Zack's smooth white fingers.

'Don't go just yet, Anya. People are looking at us. If you go now they'll think we've had a lovers' quarrel.'

Anya gave a little gasp of exasperation and withdrew her hand from his.

She glanced around and saw that a few people were eyeing them with indulgent amusement and at that moment she wondered how much of her anger was showing on her face.

'I have a childish sense of humour,' he admitted with a degree of humility she distrusted. 'Can you forgive me? Let's start again as if we've just met.'

Anya sank down into the chair again. It was too early to return to the villa anyway and there was something about this man that intrigued her.

'For a visitor you seem to be acquainted with a great many people,' she said, a little resentfully.

'I'm a friendly fellow.'

'You've come an awful long way just for a holiday.'

'I suppose so. It's a long time since I've indulged myself in this way.'

He gulped down the last of his vermouth and his lips were tight. Suddenly he looked older, far more mature.

'Indulged yourself,' she echoed. 'That's

an odd way of talking about a holiday.'

He stared down at the table top. 'Let's say I've had other things to do.' He looked up at her again. 'You seem to be on your own quite a lot. Yesterday, today. Doesn't anyone ever keep you company?'

Anya's eyes narrowed against the brightness of the sea. 'I like my own company — sometimes. Zack is always writing. He wants to finish the play before September so he keeps himself and his secretary busy, although even when she has free time Althea and I haven't much in common . . . ' except Zack, she added to herself. She sighed. 'And then there's Zack's mother . . . '

'You don't like her.'

Anya hated herself for making her feelings so obvious, but then she had never been very good at hiding them. She looked down at her hands which were clasped demurely in her lap.

'She didn't approve of Zack's marriage to my sister.' Anya looked at him then and wondered why she was saying so much to this stranger about whom she knew nothing. Perhaps, she mused, it was because he was a stranger. It was often easier than confiding in a friend, and everyone needed to confide sometimes. 'She believed he could have done much better — financially and socially.'

'It's a common disease — aspirationitis, it's called. There's no cure. The sufferer always has to go on to greater glory. We all suffer from it in varying degrees. After all it is the same urge that made us get up on to our hind legs.'

Anya had to laugh and then he asked, 'It bothers you, but does it bother your sister?'

She stopped laughing then. 'Marika died almost a year ago. She was drowned — out there somewhere.'

When she looked at him his eyes were clouded. 'I don't seem to be able to say a dozen words to you without putting my foot in it.'

'I don't mind talking about Marika. It doesn't hurt, any more than just thinking about her does.'

'It's a great tragedy. Was she a poor swimmer? The sea hereabouts is supposed to be fairly safe.'

'She was quite competent,' Anya answered, fingering her sunglasses. 'But there was a storm just after she went out. They found her the next morning, over there, washed up on that little islet.'

His eyes followed hers to the rocky little islet out in the bay. 'The storm must have taken her by surprise.'

She looked at him wide-eyed. There were lines around the corners of his mouth and he looked older again. Anya thought he would probably look the same thirty years from now.

'No, it didn't. That was the awful thing.' His eyes narrowed slightly. 'Her mother-in-law warned her there was a storm coming up and assumed that she'd not go down to the beach. I can't imagine why she did.'

'And you think that her mother-in-law could have done more to save her, don't you, Anya? That's behind this antagonism.'

'No!' Anya gasped. 'Helen wasn't to know . . .'

He said nothing for a moment and then, 'They had children, didn't they? I've seen them around.'

'Yes, Penny and Jason.' Her voice was warmer now. 'I look after them sometimes when Cèlie has time off. I enjoy that.'

His eyes widened and rolled expressively. 'Ah, Cèlie.'

His hands sketched an outline of the girl's well-endowed shape and Anya was irritated with him again. For a short while she had actually liked him.

'You know her?'

'When she has free time she usually comes to St. Brilac. She's not a girl a man could miss.'

Anya thought of Cèlie and her long dark hair, her full red lips. No, indeed a man could not miss her, especially a man like Jared Nolan.

'She's just with us until September.

She's going to college then and wants to improve her English while she's with us.' She hesitated. 'When she leaves I shall probably stay on to look after the children.'

It was the first time Anya had put her thoughts into words, but she knew the idea was in Zack's mind too. Helen would oppose it in a roundabout way but Anya was prepared for that and she didn't mind. Helen had no real affection for her grandchildren, but Anya loved them and their welfare was of prime importance to her. They would have a settled background; Anya would see to that.

'You don't look like a nursemaid.'

'You mean, I don't look like Cèlie,' she amended.

He laughed. 'Your brother-in-law might marry again. It might cause problems for you.'

A little smile played around the corners of her lips. 'I shall face that when it happens.' She looked up at him and her smile grew wider. 'And I'm sure it will.'

He looked vaguely puzzled. He couldn't understand why she was not upset at the thought. But, then, he didn't know . . .

Still feeling bright and cheery she asked, 'Which part of Canada do you come from . . . Jared?'

He looked startled. She was glad. She enjoyed surprising him out of his complacent bonhomie.

'Oh . . . er . . . Quebec.'

'That's the old part, isn't it?'

'Some of it is old and very French, and some of it is sparklingly new.' He hesitated a moment. 'It must be nice staying at the villa . . . '

'Yes, it is. Zack bought it three years ago with the fruits of his success. He has a small flat in London to use when he's there, but he prefers to live here most of the year, and I, for one, can't blame him.'

He was obviously not prepared to talk about himself and normally it would be flattering to have someone take an interest in her, if she hadn't been sure his interest was purely mercenary. Anyone could be forgiven for believing she was one of the Idle Rich.

Once again she gathered up her belongings. 'I must go now, Mr. Nolan. Thank you so much for . . . '

He got to his feet. 'You were calling me Jared a moment ago. I prefer it.'

'Very well.' She could not help the stiffness creeping into her voice. There was something off-putting about his easy familiarity. She couldn't help remembering how he had first seen her. 'Thank you for the drink.'

'I hope I shall be allowed to buy you another before long. Which way do you go back?'

Anya thought he meant to accompany her and she was determined not to allow it. She stiffened perceptibly as she answered, 'Through the wood and along the beach.' She smiled slightly. 'The way you came yesterday. As you probably realise, it's quicker that way.'

His face darkened 'I wish you wouldn't.'

'I beg your pardon!'

'I'm sorry; I *am* being presumptuous, but someone ... a girl ... was murdered in the wood last year and the murderer was never found.'

Anya stared at him hard. 'Are you joking?' She knew, of course, that he wasn't. 'I ... didn't know. Who was she?'

'A visitor. A camper. They did say a tramp was seen in the area at about that time but no one is sure. That's why ... '

Anya was thinking of that strange feeling she'd had as she walked through the wood. She shivered again.

'It must have been just about the time Marika died. That's why I didn't know. I was in England at the time it happened. We weren't very much aware of anything that went on elsewhere. How awful it is. When the sun shines so much, where there's so much natural beauty, it's hard to imagine such ugliness.'

'I didn't mean to upset you, only to warn you.' He eyed her keenly. 'I have the feeling that you usually act before you think. It's as well to think sometimes.'

Anya drew herself up and took a deep breath. For some reason she found it difficult to look at him.

'It was thoughtful of you to mention it, but whoever did that awful thing is probably miles away now, perhaps even out of the country.'

He pushed his chair away so it scraped against the ground. 'I'm sure you're right, but even so . . . '

'I *will* take care, Jared,' she said firmly, trying to push all thoughts of the crime from her mind. Murder was so commonplace nowadays. There were other kinds of tragedies too. 'And now I must go.'

'I'll walk with you to the end of the quay, if I may.' Her hesitation must have been very evident, for he added,

'I'm not setting myself up as a watchdog. Just to the end of the quay.'

She smiled and nodded and they walked along the quay by the assortment of boats which were bobbing up and down gently on the water. A girl wearing a yellow bikini, who was sunbathing on the deck of one, rather sumptuous, cruiser, shouted Jared's name as they approached and waved to him. He grinned and waved back.

Anya stopped abruptly and turned to him, considering him carefully. 'I have the oddest feeling you have a wife back home.'

He threw back his head and laughed. 'I wonder what has caused you to have such a bad opinion of married men, but as far as I'm concerned Anya, you're totally wrong. If I had a wife she'd be right here with me. Once I'm married that's how it's going to be.'

She cast him a disbelieving look. 'In the very few days you say you've been here you've made the acquaintance of a remarkable number of females.'

'That's quite natural, you know.'

'I hate to think of the legions of poor females who are weeping for your absence right now in Quebec.'

'You flatter me, but I admit it is good to get away from them for a while — a short while anyway!'

'Get away! Do you know that for someone like you coming here is very much like a mouse taking a holiday in a cheese factory?'

'I intend to eat myself sick,' he said, keeping his face straight.

Anya burst out laughing. 'I give in.'

'Good. Will you come out in the boat with me tomorrow?''

'No!'

'I mean it.' He put his right hand over his heart. 'I promise to behave myself. You have the wrong impression of me. After your little exhibition yesterday I don't know how you can accuse *me*.'

Anya was still laughing. 'Are you sure you can fit me into your schedule?'

'It's quite full but there is a vacancy

tomorrow. I'll cook lunch for you in the galley and we'll sail to Ste Marguerite afterwards.'

'One of the Lerins Isles?' He nodded and she gave a snort of derision. 'Can't you do better than that? Everyone knows it's the local lovers' lane.'

His eyes widened in mock surprise. 'Anya, I want to see the old fort. It has a fascinating history.'

Anya suddenly thought of Zack ensconced in his study all day with Althea close by. Althea and her eyes that all but devoured Zack. Althea and Zack together, shutting her out.

She looked out to sea.

'I'm not cordon bleu standard,' he said, 'but I'll cook you a passable meal; I promise not to capsize the boat and I won't make a pass at you unless you actually ask me too. Is it a date?'

She nodded. 'Yes, it's a date. I'll look forward to it.'

'Where shall we meet? Here?'

'Why not sail round the headland and I'll swim out to the boat?'

'Are you sure you want to?'

Anya was suddenly excited. He had been right; now she realised it, she had missed companionship at the villa. It was so different to her busy life in London.

'Yes, it'll be fun. I'll bring a pair of jeans and a shirt for when we go ashore.'

He held her hand briefly. 'All right, I'll meet you there at eleven o'clock. Don't be late.'

'I won't.'

He walked away a few yards and then as he had done the day before he paused to wave before striding back along the quay. Anya watched him. He waved to someone in one of the quayside cafés. A moment later a girl came running across to him. His arm fitted nicely around her waist and, laughing, the pair walked off towards his boat.

Anya drew a sigh. In all probability he would forget about tomorrow. Someone else would catch his interest before then. She turned away. She would almost be glad if it did.

3

It had rained hard all night. Anya had awoken once to hear it drumming on the flat roof of the villa. By mid-morning though there was little sign of the deluge that had been, except for a bracing of the air, which everyone welcomed.

Anya came out of the villa, welcoming the returning sun which warmed her heart and body. Once there had been a reasonable amount of lawn and shrubbery at the rear of the villa, but its situation was on the cliff edge with no extensive land attached to it, and some previous owner had sacrificed most of his lawn for a circular swimming pool. Now all that remained was a surrounding strip of lawn round the pool shaded by palms, olives, ilex trees and pines, and as many rose bushes as could be crowded into the space.

Cèlie, Anya knew, had taken the children into St. Brilac to see the boats before the heat became too great for them to be out in it. She assumed Zack would be working away at his manuscript in the study to which he had retired immediately after breakfast, but for once there was no sound of frenetic typing, so the villa was unusually quiet.

As she came out onto the patio overlooking the pool she saw Helen stretched out in a beach chair, which made her remember quite clearly what Helen had said the previous evening over dinner when Anya had deliberately mentioned her date with Jared Nolan.

'Oh dear, Anya, I do hope he's a nice person.'

Anya smiled to herself and wondered what Helen's idea of a nice person would be; a cigar-smoking, limousine-driving, jewel-spangled millionaire, she didn't doubt.

Althea had simply sniffed and said, 'There are some very unsavoury characters around St. Brilac at the moment.

They look most disreputable.'

And Zack hadn't reacted at all, for Anya had watched him closely. He had hardly paused in eating his meal and added after Althea had spoken, 'Anya is old enough to look after herself.'

Coming from anyone else she would have welcomed such words but such apparent indifference from Zack was not at all what she wished. He wasn't to know Jared was no rival.

He finished what he was eating and looked at her at last. 'Didn't you say he was from Montreal?'

'I didn't say,' she snapped, 'but he's from Quebec.'

Zack didn't reply to that. He went on eating unconcernedly until his mother started to complain about the unreliability of the local butcher, and the matter, to Anya's chagrin, was forgotten.

Anya walked as stealthily as she could without actually being on tiptoe, in the hope that Helen would not see her, but it was not to be.

As Anya attempted to retreat back into the villa she shouted across the pool, 'Going now, Anya?' There was no need for her to shout so loudly. Voices carried well in the still morning air.

'I have to change my bathing costume first. I'll be back later in the day. You'll have a quiet lunchtime today.'

Helen's brow creased. 'You *will* take care, won't you, dear?'

Her eyes opened wide. 'I always do, Helen.'

'You know what I mean.' Helen put her magazine down. 'I feel somehow responsible for you, Anya. A deputy mother, if you like.'

Anya groaned inwardly. She certainly didn't like. 'I'm used to looking out for myself,' she answered, not unkindly.

Helen laughed. 'I'm sure you are. Nevertheless . . . ' Anya pretended not to hear. She waved and hurried back into the villa and as she did so she was sure she heard Helen say, 'Poor child . . . unfortunate background.'

Anya didn't give Helen a backward

glance, but when she returned ten minutes later, clutching the waterproof bag containing her clothes, Helen's magazines were lying by the side of the chair and of the woman there was no sign. Anya was glad not to have to speak to her again and guessed that she would be in the kitchen annoying the cook, or complaining to one of the maids about a badly made bed.

She paused before going down the steps and there, sure enough, out at sea a boat was puttering round the headland. Within minutes she had reached the beach and the boat — its name — *Sea Urchin* — picked out in white on its side — was waiting within easy swimming distance in the bay.

Clutching at the oilskin bag, Anya waved and shouted Jared's name, fully expecting him to be on deck watching for her arrival.

A black-clad figure appeared on deck and Anya shouted again. He took no notice of her whatsoever although she was sure he must have both heard and seen her. She shaded her eyes with one hand against the glare of the sun and the sea. The figure bent down and when he reappeared she saw that he had an oxygen tank on. Anya stared for a moment or two, puzzled. Perhaps Jared was swimming out to meet her, but that had not been the arrangement. Even so he wasn't likely to need underwater equipment.

Anya felt a prick of unease. Whoever was on that boat was too small to be Jared Nolan. Without any further hesitation she waded into the sea and began to swim vigorously towards the *Sea Urchin*. When she had reached it she threw her bag over the side and hauled herself aboard.

'Jared . . . ' she shouted. 'I'm . . . '

Her voice tailed away as she caught sight of him. Her heart constricted with fear. He was lying senseless at the other side of the deck. She rushed over to him, calling his name over and over again, even though she knew he could not hear her. When she reached him she could see the ugly red bump on one side of his temple near the hair line. Automatically she knelt down and felt his pulse, which, to her relief, was strong.

The sea water she was dripping all over him roused him slightly and made him groan. Then he opened his eyes and would have sat up if she hadn't restrained him.

'What happened?' he asked in bewilderment, glancing around him as if he wasn't quite sure even where he was.

'I don't know, Jared. I found you like this a moment ago.'

He sat up then and groaned, burying his head in his hands. 'Something hit me but I can't for the life of me remember what. Perhaps I lost my footing.'

'The deck's dry,' she answered, 'but there was someone else on the boat with you. I saw him from the shore. Didn't you see anyone? It shouldn't be difficult in an empty sea.'

He gave a harsh laugh. 'One hardly

expects a mugging on the open sea. I seem to recall seeing a shadow . . . and then midnight.'

'Well, I did see someone, and it certainly wasn't you.'

He looked up sharply and winced as he did so. 'Who was it?'

'I couldn't tell from the shore. It was someone in a diving suit. It could have been anyone — male or female. He must have jumped overboard when he saw me.'

'It's as well you were a little early.' He smiled slightly. 'You must have been keen to come. I'm flattered.' She watched him worriedly as he moved his head and winced again. 'Ouch! That hurts.'

'It serves you right for being flippant.'

'I remember something now; when he hit me I'd just come out of the cabin.' Anya's eyes followed the trail his feet had made on the highly polished deck and then her eyes met his again. 'Anya, I've got this horrible feeling he — or she — was trying to drag me over the side. It's as well I'm a strapping fellow or you might just have been too late.'

She stared at him. 'But why would anyone want to do this to you? Are you carrying a lot of money, Jared?'

He laughed again. 'If fat pickings are what he was after, there are hundreds of millionaires' yachts in this area. This isn't anything like the Onassis yacht — or even slightly opulent. Only a maniac would think otherwise.'

'But *you* have no crew and no guards; they have them on big yachts.' She considered him for a moment or two. 'I think we'd best make for St. Brilac and find a doctor for you.'

'No need. Apart from a cracking headache, I'm all right.'

He began to get up and Anya held on to him as he swayed precariously on his feet. 'Look, I was nursing for two years — not a particularly good nurse, I admit, but I do know that the effects of a head injury such as yours can often be delayed.'

He grinned but still held on to her for support. 'Your concern is welcome, nursie, but one of the outstanding characteristics of my family is the possession of an extra thick skull. It saved my great-grandfather a scalping by Indians in the bad old days.'

It was almost a relief to have him back in his usual bantering form, except that it still annoyed her. 'You don't know what you're talking about.'

By the time they had reached the cabin and he was sitting on one of the bunks, he didn't need her inadequate support and she was more or less certain he was not concussed. Her two years of nursing had taught her something. It was obvious he had been hit only hard enough to stun him. She shuddered at the thought of what might have happened if she hadn't arrived so promptly.

Jared must have noticed her involuntary shudder, for he said quite kindly, 'Why not make us both some coffee? We both need it. And you'll find some aspirins in the first aid box in the galley. A couple of those will put me back in shape in no time at all.'

She hesitated a moment, staring at him thoughtfully, and then said, 'Why, Jared? Why would anyone want to do this to you?'

He buried his head in his hands. 'Your guess is as good as mine. Mistaken identity perhaps. I've only been here a week, which isn't long enough to make enemies. On the other hand, there are some people who believe Americans and Canadians are *all* millionaires. That could be the answer.'

'Are you going to report it to the police?'

When he looked up at her she could almost believe he was angry. 'No, I'm not! What point would there be in getting tied up in a load of French red tape when there isn't a ghost of a chance of finding out who did it? Ninety-five per cent of the population must either own or have access to diving gear and oxygen tanks. To be honest, Anya, if I didn't have you as a witness I wouldn't have believed it possible myself.'

Anya gave him a worried, timorous smile and he added, smiling back at her, 'Go on, get that coffee. No one will attack me while you're gone.'

Instead of going immediately into the galley, Anya went back on deck to retrieve her bag and automatically glanced all around. There were other boats and yachts in the vicinity but naturally there was now no sign of Jared's attacker. By now he would be safely ashore at one of the many coves which abounded along this coast.

When she went back into the cabin he was still sitting on the edge of the bunk, holding onto it as if he were afraid he might fall off.

'Did you see him?' he asked, grinning at her again.

'I went to get my clothes,' she snapped.

'You look much better as you are.'

She didn't trouble to answer him. She passed through into the tiny galley and while she was waiting for the water to boil she took off her bathing costume, dried herself thoroughly and put on her jeans and suntop, half-expecting at any time that Jared would come bursting in on her. He wasn't the type of man to consider normal conventions.

But when she went back into the cabin he was not there; she found him sitting on the deck, hugging his knees and staring out to sea. His face was set into an uncompromisingly grim expression and his complexion no longer had a healthy hue to it; he was deathly pale, and for some reason it shocked her. He was vulnerable and human, whereas she had somehow imagined him to be invincible.

When he heard her come out on deck he smiled, transforming his face once again. He eyed her low-cut suntop and jeans, saying mischievously, 'You've changed after all.'

'Any objections?'

She put the tray on the deck and squatted down beside him.

'Every objection, but you'll do.' He swallowed the aspirins and then his coffee. 'Well, whatever else you can do, Miss Kovacks, you can certainly make good coffee.'

She smiled sadly. 'I'm glad I'm not altogether hopeless at everything.' Before he could question her on that, as she knew he would like to, she went on quickly, 'We English aren't supposed to be able to make coffee at all.'

'I wouldn't agree,' he mused, 'and I doubt, with a name like Anya Kovacks, that you are English.'

She gave a little laugh. 'I am now, although Marika and I were born in Hungary, but I don't remember that part of my life at all. Just before the revolution our parents had us smuggled out of Hungary to England where my aunt had lived for some years. My parents were actively involved in the coming revolution and they stayed on to fight, obviously hoping that when it was over and they were victorious Marika and I could return to them. But everyone knows what happened. We never saw them or heard from them again. They must have had a remarkable capacity for dreaming ever to imagine they could win.'

A moment of silence hung between them and then he asked, 'Did your aunt look after you both?'

'Oh yes. She was glad to, luckily for us. She'd married well so she could support us along with her own three children. We were never sated by luxury but we did have a comfortable and happy childhood. Marika stayed there until she married Zack and I stayed on until I went to work in the hospital as a student nurse. Two of my cousins are married so Aunt Anna has only one of us at home. She enjoyed having a large family. I think she misses us now.'

Anya noticed that the colour had returned to his cheeks. He looked almost like his old self. She got to her feet and brushed off the seat of her jeans.

'I'm sorry,' he said suddenly, 'this wasn't what I'd planned for us today.'

She smiled reassuringly. 'Unless you hit yourself on the head, Jared, there's no need for you to apologise.' Her eyes met his momentarily and she was reminded of how frank they were. Then she said briskly, 'I'll take the beakers and wash them, and then bring my bathing costume out here to dry.'

As she went back into the cabin she knew he was watching her thoughtfully. For a second she felt the chill of apprehension. Perhaps he suspected her of that treacherous attack. The feeling went as fleetingly as it had come and when she came back on deck a few moments later he was in the cockpit studying some charts.

'Put your costume on the roof of the cabin,' he told her without looking round. 'And come up and join me.'

'How's the head?' she asked as she climbed up beside him.

He smiled at her. 'It's shrunk back to its normal size but I doubt if you'd notice.'

Anya could hardly repress her own smile. 'You should sit down, you know.'

Obediently he did so and she perched on the co-pilot's seat. 'I must obey my nurse,' he murmured. He glanced at her. 'Do you really think it worthwhile to give up your career in nursing to look after your sister's children?'

Anya was momentarily startled and then she looked away. 'I haven't given it up, Jared. It gave me up.'

'The work too hard for you?' He glanced at her again.

'No! I enjoyed the work, both physical and mental. I enjoyed every moment of it — or nearly every moment.'

He rolled up the charts. 'Sorry,' he said with a smile. 'It's just that I thought nursing was one of those careers one couldn't give up.'

'As I said, it gave me up.'

'What did you do? Dally with

Matron's boyfriend?'

'Certainly not.' She was looking out to sea, hating him for being so flippant about something that had caused her so much anguish.

He was watching her with a pair of grey eyes filled with amusement, but when he spoke his voice was gentle. 'I'm known as a good listener; want to tell me about it?'

Anya's head came up proudly. 'Why not? I have nothing to be ashamed of. I was always getting emotionally involved with the patients and their problems. It's just not allowed.'

His eyes narrowed slightly. 'I should have thought it was an occupational hazard.'

'So it is. Student nurses are often like that at first and they're allowed a certain amount of leeway, but in the end I wasn't getting over it and I was told I was not detached enough to make a good nurse. It was all right if the patient recovered or if there were no hard circumstances at home, but if not . . . well, I was more trouble than they could handle. I took it too much to heart. I wasn't willing to take the disappointments along with the successes.'

He put his arm around her shoulders. 'Well, cheer up. It's not the end of the world.'

She looked at him resentfully, hating his big-brother attitude almost as much as his continual bantering. 'How would you like it if it had happened to you?'

His smile faded. 'Not very much, I agree, but you'll get married one day and have a brood of kids to nurse along, including your sister's, I don't doubt. You'll end up like Aunt Anna.'

'Yes,' she murmured, 'unless . . . ' Unless Zack doesn't want me after all, she was about to say. It was possible. She looked up at him, determined not to dwell on such depressing thoughts. 'What do you do, anyway, Jared, apart from loaf around on a boat? Or do you do that all the time?'

He was handling the charts again.

'You'll be surprised to learn that I'm not the irresponsible layabout you believe me to be.'

'If you're not,' she answered dryly, 'you're in the minority in these parts. Apart from the local inhabitants most of the people you'll meet are the idle rich and those living off them — me included.'

He looked at her again and he was serious for once. 'I don't believe that for one minute, Anya.'

She looked away from him in confusion. A moment later she said, 'I bet you're an artist, going from place to place selling your paintings for just enough to live on.'

Unexpectedly he threw back his head and laughed. He caught her by the shoulders and kissed her on the cheek.

'Anya, you're a gem! I *do* wear a collar and a tie sometimes, you know.'

She was vexed again. 'You're always talking in riddles. You know almost everything there is to know about me, but I know nothing about you. I don't call that fair, Jared, do you?'

He looked at her soberly. 'Would it help you to know that I spend most of my time rescuing erring citizens of Quebec from the clutches of the law? As in your job, Anya, sometimes I'm successful and sometimes not, only *I* try not to take it to heart.'

He let her go. 'You're a lawyer,' she said, falling back against the rail. 'That's something I never would have guessed.'

He laughed again. 'I'm on holiday, strictly off duty. I've left my wing collar back in Quebec, so if you have any legal problems take them elsewhere.'

'You're rude,' she protested.

'I didn't mean to be. Anyway, I'm only a very junior partner in my firm and I only know Canadian law.' He was looking past her, to the shore. 'We're being watched. Did you know?'

Anya swung round and saw that someone was watching them through binoculars from the garden of the Villa Donmarie. The sun glinted off the glass for a moment or two and then disappeared.

Anya turned away again. Jared's eyes were narrow slits and then he looked at her. She felt guilty, although reason told her she had no reason to be.

'Have you any idea who that might be?'

'How could I? It could be anyone. Zack has a pair of powerful field glasses and I'm always seeing them around. Anyone can use them. I've used them myself on occasions. Even Jason has a little pair of his own.'

Jared let out a deep sigh. 'Oh, well, it doesn't really matter; they're not going to see any wild orgies going on here.'

'Why not?' she asked, suddenly mischievous. So far it hadn't proved to be a very enjoyable morning.

'I *knew* you were abandoned,' he said triumphantly. 'I think I'm going to move this ship to where no one can see us.' Anya laughed and he looked down at her from what seemed to be a great height. 'How about lunch, Anya? I'm starving.'

She looked at him doubtfully. 'Are you sure you're all right? I would prefer you to put into shore and see a doctor — just in case. It would be sensible.'

He put his hands on her shoulders and looked down into her eyes. If Zack were in his place she would be trembling now.

'I'm sensible forty-eight weeks in the year, so I'm allowing myself four weeks of being a little foolish if I feel like it.'

'Seriously, Jared!' she protested.

'I'm perfectly all right now, thanks to Nurse Kovacks' treatment,' he answered mildly. 'I know I promised to make lunch, but can you cope as well with a can opener? I've got a good selection of canned food in the galley and in my state of health I can't be expected to make lunch.'

His eyes gleamed with amusement. Anya knew there was nothing more she could do. If the stubborn creature keeled over with delayed shock at some later stage it wouldn't be her fault.

'When it comes to cooking out of tins I'm in the cordon bleu class,' she answered with a degree of flippancy she felt he would appreciate at that moment.

He smiled back at her. 'I knew you would be when I asked you yesterday.'

'You're unprincipled, Jared. I bet you contrive to get yourself looked after all the time.'

'Most of the time,' he admitted, adding as she was about to enter the cabin again, 'Anya, I'd be grateful if you'd not mention this . . . accident of mine to anyone.'

She paused. 'But it wasn't an accident . . . '

His request had been made in a gentle voice, but behind it was a hint of steel. This man was something of an enigma to her. He was so easy-going and casual and yet Anya was convinced there was more than that in his nature. He would have to be hard and calculating at times to succeed in his career, but try as she would she just could not imagine Jared Nolan sitting behind a desk in an office or standing before a judge and jury, perhaps defending a man against a lifetime of imprisonment.

He was very well aware of her hesitation. 'Please, Anya.'

She nodded. 'If that's what you want.'

'I do.'

She added in desperation, 'You're very stubborn.'

He smiled at her and he was himself again. 'That's my middle name.'

He climbed down from the cockpit with all the ease of a seasoned mariner. Anya studied him carefully for a moment or two. 'Doesn't *anything* bother you, Jared?' she asked.

Momentarily he was serious. 'Oh yes, Anya. Some things do.' Then he tapped her lightly on the behind. 'Go on inside, galley slave, your master's starving and if he doesn't get his food he's likely to turn nasty. After the splendid meal I know you're going to cook for me, I'm going to take you to Ste Marguerite!'

Anya was still chuckling when she went into the galley and started to prepare a meal in the most cramped conditions she had ever known. Jared's attacker was almost forgotten, and she had certainly forgotten that her acceptance of his invitation was an attempt to make Zack jealous. The very thought of it seemed childish now, and she had discovered that Jared Nolan was too nice a person to be used in that way.

She could hear him moving about on deck and as the eggs began to sizzle in the pan, Anya started to hum a happy little song. Perhaps the day would turn out nicely after all.

4

Anya stood by the patio windows looking out into the inky blackness of the night. As she caught sight of her reflection in the partially open window she wondered, had he been there, if Jared would recognise her. The long white silk evening dress made her look taller, older, more of a woman.

'Your coffee's getting cold, Anya,' Helen reminded her and Anya turned reluctantly and went back into the room.

She was delightfully aware of Zack's eyes following her as she crossed the room.

'There you are, dear,' said Helen, handing her the cup, 'good and strong, just as you like it.'

Helen's eyes, dark like her son's, were bright with the questions she would like to have asked. Since her return late that afternoon Anya had made no mention of her outing with Jared Nolan.

It was Zack who at last asked, 'Did you have an enjoyable day out, Anya?'

His high cheek bones cast curious hollows in his face and his eyes were as always fathomless. Anya realised for the first time that it was always impossible to divine what he was really thinking.

She stirred her coffee and answered in as casual a voice as she could manage. 'Couldn't you tell yourself while you were watching us through your field glasses, Zack?'

'Me? Why on earth would I do that? I was hard at work all day, let me tell you, not gallivanting around in a boat.' His voice softened with satisfaction. 'As a matter of fact I had a very good day. I kept poor Althea hard at the grind with only a short break for lunch, so whoever it was, Anya, it certainly wasn't me.'

Althea smiled superciliously. 'I don't mind, Zack. It's what I'm paid for; I don't want to do anything else. In fact,

I must admit, I feel . . . honoured.' She gave an embarrassed little laugh. 'It's splendid seeing your work coming on so well. At one time I thought . . . '

'We won't talk about it any more,' he said gently. 'It's sufficient that this play is going to be better than any of the others.'

'That's certainly saying something,' murmured Anya, feeling that some such sentiment should be voiced.

'I am glad,' said his mother, sighing contentedly. She looked at Anya again; she was still stirring her coffee and had not yet drunk one drop of it. 'You're probably mistaken, dear. I'm sure no one here would be watching you. Why should they?'

'That's what I wondered,' she murmured, almost to herself.

Althea helped herself to a cigarette from the box on the table in front of her, and Zack jumped up immediately to light it for her. Anya watched them, so did Helen and they both felt similar sentiments. Helen, Anya knew, would not like Zack to marry Althea any more than she would. Helen wouldn't want him to marry anyone.

Althea looked up into his eyes and smiled her thanks in a particularly intimate way. Zack sat down again and lit a cheroot for himself. He blew a long column of smoke into the air.

What an ill-assorted group we are, Anya thought; we have only one thing in common — our devotion to Zack.

'We sailed to Ste. Marguerite,' she said, breaking the silence that was becoming oppressive. Somehow she couldn't rid herself of the peculiar sensation that someone at Villa Donmarie had been watching her and Jared on *Sea Urchin*. There was nothing odd about looking out to sea through field glasses; the odd part was that no one would admit to it.

'I thought there was nothing on the island but trees,' said Althea with a mild show of interest.

'That's what I thought too,' answered Anya, 'until Jared . . . ' Zack was watching her and she blushed a little, ' . . . reminded me that there was a fort that was once the prison of the Man in the Iron Mask.'

Zack slapped the arm of his chair. 'Of course! I should have remembered that.' He flicked a long column of ash from his cheroot and glanced at his mother. 'Do you know, Mother? He was imprisoned there for seventeen years and no one today knows for certain who he really was.'

'How fascinating,' Helen answered, pouring another cup of coffee for herself and Althea. She looked a little more than bored at the aesthetic turn of the conversation. 'I believe I saw a film about him once.'

Althea crushed out her cigarette. 'There's a very popular rumour that he may have been the illegitimate brother of Louis the Fourteenth.'

'We'll never know,' murmured Zack.

'And really,' added Helen, laughing, 'does it matter?'

'Jared has heard another rumour.'

They all looked at Anya. She popped a chocolate into her mouth, enjoying being the centre of Zack's attention.

'Well, don't keep us in suspense,' he said in an amused voice.

'Apparently the man was provided with a mistress to help him while away the time.'

Althea laughed and Zack said languidly, 'I should think he'd need something. I'd go mad even with such privileges.'

'Well,' Anya went on, 'the rumour has it that they had a child who was taken away and *entrusted* to foster parents in Corsica.'

Zack's eyes sparkled. 'I have a feeling there's a point to this story.'

Anya swallowed another fondant cream. 'There certainly is; entrusted translated into French is *remis de bonne part* and in Italian *di buona parte.*'

'Bonaparte,' said Althea, sitting forward. 'What a fascinating idea.'

'If the prisoner was indeed related to

the King,' Anya reasoned, 'and this child was Napoleon's great-grandfather, then Napoleon wasn't just the peasant everyone believed him to be. He did have a claim to the throne of France.'

'He was still a scoundrel,' said Zack, scowling. He got to his feet. 'I'm glad you've found a friend, Anya, and I'm pleased that you've enjoyed yourself today. Next time visit St. Honorat; it's even more deserted.' He smiled. 'It makes for togetherness. Come, Althea, we still have work to do tonight. Excuse us, won't you?'

Althea murmured, 'Good night,' as she quickly followed her employer from the room.

Anya watched them go, feeling something like dismay. She had always been aware of Althea's attachment to Zack but once again she could see how well suited they were; for the first time she was uneasy about their relationship; for the first time she felt totally shut out, and it frightened her.

Suddenly she was aware that Helen

was speaking to her. She turned and smiled weakly. 'I'm sorry, Helen, you'll have to excuse me too. I'm tired. A little too much of the sun and the sea today, I dare say. I think I'll go to bed now.'

She hurried out of the salon, not caring if Zack's mother did consider her rude. She paused outside Zack's study but no light showed beneath the door and unashamedly she listened to hear any sound from within, but there was none.

Anya went slowly up the curved marble staircase. Her own room was at the end of the corridor, almost opposite the nursery suite occupied by Cèlie and the children. The door was open a shade and a light shone through. She hesitated and then on impulse knocked softly.

Cèlie was sprawled across the pink counterpane, her cheeks cupped in her hands. She sprang up as Anya came in. 'Good evening, Miss Kovacks,' she said, smiling with genuine pleasure and brushing back her heavy curtain of dark hair.

'How are the children? Did they enjoy their trip to St. Brilac?'

'Oh, they are fine. Such good children. Monsieur Guidet gave them a short ride around the bay in his motor boat and they enjoyed that very much.' She looked at Anya with a calculating eye. 'Did you also enjoy your boat trip, mam'selle?'

'Yes, it was very nice,' Anya answered quickly, and then, moving towards the children's room, she asked, 'May I look in on Penny and Jason?'

'But of course, Miss Kovacks.'

Anya tiptoed into the children's room. Penny still slept in a cot and Jason in a small bed nearby. As she bent over first one and then the other they smelled sweet and fresh from their baths. As she straightened up she had a lump in her throat. The early upheavals in her own life had not been allowed to affect her adversely and she was determined that these little ones should also have a settled future. She loved Zack and she loved the children; what better course was there than for them to marry? But when she thought of Althea, Anya knew that she was determined too, and she felt chill.

She turned round to find Cèlie standing in the doorway watching her. Anya smiled and quickly went back into the other room.

'Your English has improved enormously, Cèlie, since you came to us.'

The girl lowered her eyes demurely. 'I am glad to hear you say so, mam'selle. That was my intention. My stay here has been most beneficial.'

'May I sit down?'

'Of course.' Cèlie sank back into the bed and patted the counterpane. 'Please do sit down. It is kind of you to come.'

She pulled at the hem of her skirt in an effort to pull it further down her thighs but there was still a large expanse of firm tanned flesh to be seen. Cèlie was always in the background, never thrusting herself forward, and yet one had to notice her. She exuded a quiet kind of sexuality which disturbed Anya somehow.

'I'm looking forward to being with the children tomorrow, when it's your day off. Do you find it hard to keep occupied away from the villa?'

Cèlie's deep blue eyes opened ingenuously. 'I have made lots of friends in St. Brilac. I shall be visiting some tomorrow.'

Anya recalled Jared's knowing smile as he mentioned Cèlie's name and she wondered if he were one of the friends she was speaking of. Glancing at the girl's face, her half smile, the knowing secretive smile of the Mona Lisa, Anya knew that Cèlie would not be telling.

'Tell me something, Cèlie,' Anya said thoughtfully a moment later, 'do you recall those toy field glasses Jason was bought some time ago?'

'Yes, mam'selle. He treasures them. He carries them with him all the time. He looks at everything through them, even objects quite close by.'

Anya leaned forward eagerly. 'Ah, I thought I saw him when I was on Mr. Nolan's boat. He was watching us, up by the wall on the cliff.'

Cèlie's secret little smile faded. 'Oh no, Miss Kovacks! The children are never allowed near the edge of the cliff. Besides, we were in St. Brilac all morning and after lunch the children and myself rested in here.'

Who on earth had it been then? Anya asked herself. She had never really believed it to be Jason anyway. Helen, Althea, Zack, even Cèlie. One of them had almost certainly been watching her, and one of them was not admitting it.

Anya forced a smile to her lips. 'Yes, I realise that now. It was foolish of me to forget.'

There was a magazine lying open on the bed which the girl had been reading when Anya had disturbed her. Anya picked it up, glad of an excuse to change the subject.

'What are you reading? Anything exciting?'

Cèlie looked abashed. 'Just a little escapism.'

Anya glanced at the cover; it was a lurid magazine purporting to report true life crimes. Anya turned back to the page Cèlie had been reading and found herself looking into the laughing eyes of a dark haired girl, very attractive and so vivacious Anya could almost feel her personality emerge from the paper.

She stared at the picture for a moment or two and then said, 'She doesn't look like a criminal to me, but I suppose one can never tell.'

Cèlie looked a little embarrassed before answering in a hushed voice, 'She is not a criminal, mam'selle. It is an awful thing that happened. Her name is Paulette Duvaloir, a student like me.' Her voice became even more hushed. 'She was murdered — strangled — in the St. Brilac wood only last year.'

Anya stared at the photograph of the alive face of Paulette Duvaloir, and then closed the magazine. 'I had heard about the crime,' she answered stiffly, unable to get that laughing face out of her mind. 'But I didn't know who was the victim.' She got to her feet, anxious to be away now. 'I won't keep you up any longer, Cèlie. I'll see you in the morning.'

The girl stood up too. 'It's upsetting, isn't it? Knowing such a horrible crime was committed so close. The murderer was never found. One could meet him every day and not know it.'

Anya nodded slowly as she paused in the doorway and shivered slightly. The victim had been just a victim before, easy to forget, but now she had a name and a face, and Anya had the strangest feeling it was going to haunt her.

5

'How lucky can one man get? I've actually got you to myself for once.'

Anya looked up from the book she was reading and into Zack's smiling face. He was wearing a white beach-robe over a pair of swimming trunks. He looked so tanned and handsome her heart missed a beat.

She put the book down and stood up slowly. 'Aren't you working?'

He drew a sigh. 'I've done a good day's writing already. Mother and Althea have gone to have their hair done, and I reckon I'm due for some time off too.'

She sat down again and he sank down on to the edge of the beach chair, very close to her. Her head swam dangerously. Althea and Helen were out and Cèlie was once more in charge of the children. Zack was hers for now, be it only for an hour.

He stared into the clinically blue depths of the pool for a moment and then covered her hand firmly with his.

'This is a lonely summer for you, Sweetie. You must miss Marika.'

Her heart constricted and her eyes clouded with the pain of it. 'It's worse for you and the children. Far worse.'

He smiled sadly. 'The children will grow up and forget, if they haven't forgotten already, and I have my work, thank heavens.'

'Is it going well?' she asked eagerly.

'Very well. I thought for a while, after Marika died, I was finished for good, but this, I think, is going to be a good one — the best perhaps. I feel it in my bones.'

'Oh, I am glad, Zack. It's some consolation even though it's not much.'

He turned away. 'I'm only sorry you have so much of your time taken up with minding the children. You're not to be here as nursemaid.'

'I love the children, Zack. I love being

with them. They are part of me too, you know. It's no chore I promise you.'

He smiled and looked at her again. 'But you should be out with friends of your own age, Anya. If only I could get a permanent nursemaid . . . '

'You don't need one, Zack. If you agree, I'll stay on and look after them when Cèlie leaves. They're my flesh and blood and as I've said, I love them.'

'You're marvellous, Anya.' She flushed, unable to meet his gaze. 'You do mean it, don't you?'

'Of course I do, Zack.' She met his eyes then. 'And as for friends, there's no one who means more to me than you and the children.'

He brushed an insect from the sleeve of his bathrobe. 'And what about this Nolan fellow? Is there something serious there? It would be unrealistic for me to plan . . . '

Anya burst out laughing. 'Jared Nolan! You must be joking! I hardly know the man . . . and besides, he's not my type.'

'I'm relieved to hear you say it,' he grinned, looking into her eyes again. 'You've no idea how relieved.' His hand tightened on her arm. 'When this play's finished, Anya, we'll get out and about together. I'll make up for neglecting you this summer.'

'That will be marvellous,' she said breathessly. All her doubts flew away on the breeze.

She clasped her arms around her knees. 'Zack, did you hear about a murder that was committed near here last year?'

He stiffened and his eyes narrowed. 'Yes, I do remember something. The local police came around asking questions but we couldn't help at all, and then Marika died and of course we never gave it another thought. What made you mention it now?'

'They never found the person who did it. Cèlie was reading a magazine that had a story in about it. She was a very lovely girl.'

'Don't think about it, Anya,' he said

gently. 'We have our own tragedy. Marika was lovely too.'

'But murder, Zack — a deliberate act — is so horrible. The person — the animal — who did it is still free.'

'No, I doubt if he's that. The knowledge will be with him, so he can never be truly free.' Then he added more briskly, 'I forbid you to think about it any more, Sweetie. Think of now, and the future — and us.'

She smiled weakly and laid her cheek against the roughness of his robe. 'You are right, Zack, so right.'

He raised her chin and kissed her lightly on the lips. 'I hate that man for being able to spend so much of his time with you while I have to stay here working.'

Anya drew away. 'Do you mean Jared?'

'Yes, Jared, curse him.'

She chuckled. 'You're jealous.'

'He's claiming more than his fair share of your time lately.'

'Althea claims yours.'

'She's paid to.' The sparkle was back in his eyes, much to her relief. 'You're seeing him tonight again.'

She nodded complacently. 'He asked me to have dinner with him. He's hiring a car and we're driving into the hills. It will be madly romantic,' she added, trying not to laugh at so outrageous an idea as Jared Nolan being romantic.

'You little minx,' Zack grinned, 'you're doing it deliberately.'

Her eyes opened wide in innocence. 'Jared is an attractive, intelligent companion.'

'About whom you know precious little.'

'I know enough. He's a lawyer from Quebec.'

Zack looked grim. 'He's taking Cèlie for dinner tomorrow night.'

For a moment Anya was too taken aback to answer and then she said stiffly, 'He's perfectly entitled to.'

'I envy him,' he admitted. 'In fact, I'd very much like to meet this industrious fellow. Why don't you ask him to dine here one evening? After tomorrow, of course.'

Anya looked at him suspiciously. 'Do you mean it?'

'Of course I do.'

'He won't come.'

Somehow she didn't want him to. Jared wouldn't fit in at the Villa Donmarie.

'You'll never know if you don't ask him, Anya.' He hesitated before adding, 'I'll feel happier if you bring your friends up to the villa. After all, you know so little about him, if you come to think of it.'

'Don't come the Big Brother,' she teased.

'Oh, I'm not that any more, besides,' he reminded her, 'Jared Nolan isn't your type. You admitted it.'

She smiled back at him. His hand brushed a strand of hair away from her face and then the magic moment was shattered.

'Oh, so here you are.'

Zack got up quickly and swung

round to face his mother and Althea, both neatly coiffured. Anya sank back in the beach chair and forcibly stopped herself from laughing out loud. Both women had smiles on their lips but Helen's eyes were flinty as she surveyed the intimate scene she had come upon, and Althea's demeanour fairly exuded hostility.

'You both look absolutely ravishing,' Zack exclaimed, and the tightness immediately went from his mother's smile.

'I keep telling Anya she should have her hair styled properly. It would make all the difference to her appearance.'

Zack looked down at her. 'I think she looks delightful as she is.'

Anya smiled back at him gratefully. Althea sat down in a wrought iron chair nearby and crossed her legs elegantly. No lounging for Althea.

'Did they really make you cut it off?' she asked.

Anya laughed. 'No, of course not! We're not in Victorian times now. I'm just no good at keeping it tidy and a nurse must have her hair tidy.'

'What a pity your sacrifice was in vain.'

'Nothing is ever in vain,' Anya answered frostily.

Helen turned back into the villa, saying, 'I think I shall have a rest before dinner.' She looked pointedly at Anya. 'I understand you won't be joining us.'

Althea smiled. Just at that moment Anya hated her. She looked slyly from under her eyelashes. 'Anya has a date.'

Anya ignored her and answered Helen with as much civility as she could muster. 'Jared is calling for me.' She hesitated, glancing at Zack who was lounging against the trunk of a palm tree watching the three women in his life. 'Zack has asked me to invite him here.'

Helen glanced at her son. 'Really, Zack, are you sure you want to while you're working?'

Zack shrugged indolently. 'It's only right, Mother. He's Anya's friend, and it will make a pleasant change for us all to have a visitor.'

'Very well, dear,' she answered briskly and was gone, making no secret of her disapproval.

'She doesn't like me to be treated as one of the family,' Anya said bitterly.

'Nonsense,' answered Zack. 'You *are* one of the family.'

'To her I'm a foreigner, and so was Marika. She never liked or approved of us.'

Zack glanced uncertainly at Althea who was unconcernedly examining her pink-tipped nails. With no attempt to hurry she unfolded herself from the chair, saying, 'Don't worry about me. I have some letters to write before dinner.' She crossed the patio, tossing back at them, 'You two go on and argue if you like. I used to be just the same with my brother when I was a child.'

When she had gone Zack gave the trunk of the palm tree a little thump with his fist. 'I wish you wouldn't make such extravagant claims about Mother,

Anya. You know that she's very fond of you and she adored Marika.'

Anya jumped to her feet. 'You've always been like an ostrich with its head buried in the sand, Zack! Marika was a lot more easy going than I am. She could afford to be; she was married to you.'

He smiled and came towards her but she was in no mood now to be soothed. Helen Anderson had irritated her once too often.

'Come on, Sweetie, let's not quarrel.'

'There would be no need to if you saw the truth. Your mother is a snob, Zack. A good old-fashioned, dyed-in-the-wool snob. And if you don't recognise it, she's going to poison every relationship you have — even that with your own children!'

Her anger suddenly evaporated as he stared at her in stupefaction. 'It's not that she resented Marika, or Althea, or me — it's anyone who comes remotely close to you, Zack.'

His face contorted into a grimace of

fury. He caught her arm as she made to go past him. 'My life's my own, Anya,' he said furiously in her ear. She gasped in pain as his grip tightened on her arm. She had never seen him angry before. 'But just you remember that this is my mother's home too.'

The tears sprung to her eyes as he let her go, turning from her in a gesture that was more painful than any physical abuse. The colourful tableau of flowers in the tiny garden — roses, hibiscus, bougainvillaea — merged into one riotous confusion.

'Zack, I'm sorry,' she murmured through her tears.

He nodded, but said nothing. She waited for a moment or two and then he said, still without looking at her, 'Go on, Anya, or you'll be late for your date.'

'Zack, I didn't mean to make you angry.'

He turned and smiled at her. The fury was gone. Anya had never felt so relieved.

'I'm sorry too. I don't very often lose my temper but when I do it's fireworks.'

She laughed nervously and hurried back towards the house. As she entered it she heard a splash. When she reached the landing she looked out of the window and saw him ploughing through the cool water of the pool.

The sound of children's voices in the corridor made her hurry away from the window. Jason was wearing his water wings and so was Penny. Cèlie walked between them, her tiny bikini visible beneath an almost transparent wrap.

Anya was able to forget her quarrel with Zack for a few moments as she talked to the excited children. Then she straightened up again.

'Monsieur Anderson wishes the children to join him for a while before bedtime,' the girl informed her. 'They are becoming quite good swimmers.'

'Real water babies,' Anya murmured. 'Well, I won't keep you.' As they were about to pass Anya asked thoughtfully,

'I understand you're having an evening off tomorrow.'

Cèlie smiled her secret smile again. 'Yes, I am invited out by a friend.' She gave Anya a look of pure innocence. 'Monsieur Nolan. He is very nice.'

'You'd better go and join Mr. Anderson now, Cèlie,' Anya answered abruptly, hating herself for doing so. Cèlie smiled good naturedly and was gone, and along with her the children. Anya waited a moment or two and went back to the window. Cèlie, Zack and the children were playing at the shallow end of the pool, laughing and splashing. Anya felt no lift from watching what was a very natural scene. She just felt cold.

★ ★ ★

Jared followed Anya out onto the viewing platform just outside the little inn which was perched high in the Esterel mountains.

Anya, clutching a glass of brandy,

wandered across to the balustrade and gazed down to the coast where the lights of the many resorts tucked into every cove sparkled brightly, where the sea shone like silver in the moonlight.

She pulled her silk stole tighter around her as the breeze ruffled her hair.

'Not cold, are you?' he asked, leaning back against the balustrade so he could face her.

She drew a deep breath. 'No, just deliciously cool. The air is marvellous up here.'

Earlier, while speaking to Zack, Anya had jokingly taunted him, telling him how romantic this evening would be, and had she thought of Jared Nolan in such a way, romantic was exactly how this evening would be.

Anya had dismissed her earlier unhappiness during the winding climb up into the mountains in the open-topped car Jared had hired. Around them was the famed *maquis*, alive with a tapestry of colour woven by the yellow broom, white heather, and thorny cistus bushes. Now darkness had fallen and the mountains were just rugged outlines against a navy blue star-spangled night.

'Do you think there are more stars in the French heavens than anywhere else on earth, Jared?' she asked, looking upwards.

'Perhaps.'

His voice was very soft in the darkness and suddenly she was very much aware of being alone out here with him.

Unsteadily, gazing before her she said, 'It looks as though dozens of them have fallen to earth along the coast.'

'Have you never been up here before?'

She laughed and sipped at her brandy, cupping it in both hands. 'No, never. Isn't that strange?'

'These hills used to be filled with bandits at one time,' he said, glancing behind him. 'During the last war the Resistance used to hide in the *maquis*. It has quite a chequered history.'

Anya was suddenly despondent. If she were with Zack he would be trying to make love to her by now.

'No one at the villa is interested. All they want is the sea and the sun.'

'Which is very nice,' Jared pointed out.

She smiled and handed him her empty glass which he placed with his own on a nearby table. 'So it is. I love it too.'

He was looking at her steadily. 'Did you enjoy the meal?'

Anya caught her breath. 'Very much. It was perfect. I'm glad I had you to help me with the menu.'

He was still watching her. When he had called for her she was a little taken aback to see him wearing a smart suit, well-cut to fit the breadth of his muscular shoulders. All at once his personality had taken on another facet. His character gained more depth but despite her conversations with him Anya realised he was still but a stranger.

'Do you realise,' she said after a

moment, 'that this is the first time I've actually seen you wearing a suit?'

'My working clothes, actually, only I couldn't take out a lady wearing my week-end clothes.'

'I didn't mind where you took me, Jared,' she told him truthfully.

'I didn't want you to think of me as a beatnik.'

'You might have started to think *I* was a boy,' she answered with a laugh.

'Ah, impossible. You're forgetting our first meeting.'

Anya was glad the night hid her embarrassment. One hand gripped the balustrade and he put his lightly over it and laughed softly. 'I promise I won't mention it again — or at least I shall try not to.'

She withdrew her hand and he folded his arms in front of him. 'Do you remember mentioning that girl who was murdered last year?'

He straightened up slowly. His face was in shadow so she could not read his expression, but his voice was guarded as he answered softly, 'Yes, I remember.'

'I saw her photograph last night.' He reached out behind him and gripped the top of the balustrade. 'Cèlie was reading a true crime magazine and the case was reported in it. She looked so alive, so beautiful . . .'

'Would it have been any less of a crime if she'd been old and ugly, Anya?'

She looked away. 'Of course it wouldn't. It's just . . .'

'I know what you mean. When I was your age I didn't like to believe men capable of such ugliness either, but there is a dark side to human nature.' He laughed grimly. 'I've seen quite a bit of it. You'd be surprised at how many ugly deeds are done by the most unlikely people.'

'I've seen ugliness too, Jared,' she said, swallowing a lump in her throat.

She didn't quite know why this crime had affected her so. Its proximity perhaps, the fact that the victim could have been anyone — herself — or that the perpetrator could be anyone too, anyone . . .

'I've been a nurse,' she whispered.

'And that's a profession you're unsuited to, despite all your good intentions.'

'Yes,' she breathed, inhaling the sweet-scented night. It had the effect of chasing away some of the ghosts that were haunting her.

He was watching her thoughtfully and for once she was disturbed by his scrutiny. She remembered that tomorrow he would be wining and dining Cèlie; dark, sexy, secretive Cèlie with the giaconda smile. They would not spend their time talking as he and Anya were doing now. For the first time she was aware that here was a man, and, she supposed, to some women he would be every bit as attractive as Zack, with the same desires and appetites as his fellow men.

Anya gave herself a mental shake. First she had been wondering about Zack's relationship with Althea, and now she was imagining Jared and Cèlie together. She smiled to herself, thinking, 'If my own love-life was completely satisfactory I wouldn't waste my time making conjecture about everyone else's.'

'I wonder what that delightful little smile's about,' he mused, and she realised there had been quite a silence between them.

Her smile grew broader. 'I have an invitation for you; Zack would like you to come up to the villa for dinner with us one evening.'

He looked surprised and then pleased, very pleased. 'That's very kind of him. When?'

Anya smiled again, turning away slightly. 'It will have to be after tomorrow night, won't it? You're engaged elsewhere tomorrow.'

'I take it Cèlie has told you I'm taking her out.'

'She told Zack, and he told me.' She looked at him wide-eyed. 'I don't suppose it was meant to be a secret.'

'Heavens, no! She's interested in emigrating to Canada once her studies are over, and I'm going to tell her what I can about it. We'll probably have a bowl of bouillabaisse at Jules' bar.'

'So I'm honoured with all this,' she said impishly. 'The shirt and the tie.'

'If you want to think so,' he answered, a little shortly Anya thought. It pleased her to embarrass him. It made a welcome change.

More seriously she said, 'I hadn't thought of you as a career counsellor.'

'You hadn't thought of me as a lawyer either, but I am. There's lots more to me than you've seen so far.'

'I don't doubt it. Are you accepting Zack's invitation?'

Her voice was stiff. She didn't know why, but she didn't want him to accept. She didn't want him to meet Zack. She didn't want to see them together.

'Do you want me to?'

His question startled her. He could read her thoughts too accurately, too often, for comfort. 'Why shouldn't I?'

she retorted, more stiffly still.

'Then I'm delighted to accept. Will the night after tomorrow be convenient?'

'If it isn't I'll let you know.' She hesitated. 'We don't usually entertain, not while Zack is working. It's a small houseparty, too, for the same reason. His mother will be there . . . '

'The one you don't like.'

'And Althea, his secretary.'

'You don't like her either.'

His perception was beginning to annoy her. The stole had slipped from her shoulders and she shivered. He stood up and put it around her shoulders, folding it across her breasts. Anya clasped it tightly.

'You're very sensitive, Anya. It's a hard life for people like you.' He put his arm loosely around her waist and drew her back towards the inn. 'Come along inside, you're getting cold out here. We'll have more brandy and hot coffee, and you can tell me how long you've been in love with Zack Anderson . . . '

She stopped abruptly and pulled away from his encircling arm. 'What did you say?'

He was no longer flippant. His grey eyes were sombre in the pool of light shed by the windows of the old stone inn. 'I'm not wrong, am I?'

Her eyes held his for a moment and then she lowered hers. 'How did you guess?'

He laughed but there was a harsh sound to it. 'It's not difficult. It's just the way your voice softens every time you mention his name.'

There was something of relief in being able to admit it, even if it was to an outsider, someone who was entirely unbiased. She had kept the knowledge in her heart for so long.

'I was thirteen when Marika met and married Zack. I fell in love with him then. There's never been anyone else.'

'And how does he feel about you?'

Anya couldn't look at him. 'I'm not sure; Zack is charming to everyone.'

'I can understand it. A charming and

115

talented man, sophisticated. You know, Anya, Zack won't have changed at all, but you have. You're not thirteen any more. It's time to take another look at yourself.'

'Heavens,' she said irritably, 'you do see yourself as a counsellor, don't you? Well, I'll tell you something, Jared; I worked in a hospital for two years — not a convent — and I met any number of eligible men. Not one of them affected me.'

The lines on his angular face softened. 'You're a dreamer, Anya, a hero-worshipper. One life, one love. I envy him.'

Suddenly she laughed, startling him. 'He said the same of you.' When he frowned she explained. 'Because you've been seeing both Cèlie and myself at the same time. He thinks you're industrious.'

He laughed too then. 'I suppose I am. Come on inside; I think we're ready for that other brandy now.'

6

Gervase, the man who looked after the house and grounds, was cleaning the pool. Anya sat on its tiled perimeter, hugging her legs beneath her chin and watching him as he worked. It was early and the pool needed regular cleaning, but Anya wished she could go for a swim, and yet she hadn't the slightest inclination, for once, to go down to the beach.

Her mind relived time and time again last evening; the night Jared had come to dinner. To her surprise he had charmed everyone, although she knew instinctively that he and Zack did not like each other. She had known that would be so before the two men even met. Their personalities were too diverse for them to find any area of real communication; and yet the evening had been, without doubt, a success.

Althea had been more than usually pleasant and attentive to the guest, slightly less distant than usual, but, then, Anya had to remind herself, Jared was a man. He had even impressed Helen by claiming acquaintance with one or two important Canadians. Anya wasn't sure whether Jared was being serious or whether his sense of humour was again active. But he seemed perfectly sincere and Helen believed him.

Anya had watched him behave with sureness and ease amongst a group of people who, except for herself, were strangers, and she found her respect for him growing. Each time she had seen him since their first meeting he had grown in stature, and yet she was aware she still knew very little about him; she didn't need Zack's consistent reminders to appreciate that.

Eventually the conversation, as Anya somehow knew it would, came to touch on the murder that had occurred nearby the previous year. They had been talking about some of Jared's professional experiences and Zack had asked, 'How do you go about getting an acquittal for a man you know is as guilty as hell?'

Zack was smoking a long cigarette, sitting back in his chair, his dark eyes glittering with an intensity Anya could not recognise. He had spoken very little during the evening; she hoped it was a small case of jealousy on her behalf, but with Zack one never could tell.

'It depends,' Jared answered, 'whether the person is guilty or innocent.'

'But what if you know he is guilty?'

'There would be many factors to consider first. First I would have to be sure of a man's guilt or innocence before deciding how to proceed.'

Zack leaned forward. 'That isn't what I meant.'

'I know what you meant. No lawyer worth his salt would represent a guilty man as innocent. He would, instead, put forward any mitigating circumstances.'

Only one lamp was lit, casting weird

shadows in all corners of the room. Just then Zack's thin face took on a foxy look. He was testing Jared in some way, and Anya couldn't fathom why or how.

'And if there aren't any?'

'There always are,' answered Jared. 'There's usually a motive for killing for instance. No one kills without reason.'

'I disagree,' said Althea slowly. 'There are any number of motiveless killings every year.'

Jared gave her an indulgent smile. 'To the public it may appear to be so, but to the murderer himself there is always a cause, be it only in his own mind.'

At this Anya felt bound to say, and somehow felt guilty for it, 'The murder of that girl last year in the wood was considered motiveless.'

No one answered for a moment and then Althea said, 'There was talk of a lovers' quarrel.'

Jared said, 'It's unlikely anyone will know until the murderer is caught.'

'Which is unlikely after this length of time.'

It was Helen who spoke at last in a high timorous voice and it was almost a question.

'I wouldn't say that,' Jared answered thoughtfully. 'The French police are very thorough even though they may not seem to be.'

'This crime is quite a *cause celèbre* in the area,' Zack said as he leaned forward to crush out his cigarette, 'but my wife died at about the same time, so our own tragedy took all our attention.'

'Oh, don't let's talk about such horrible things!' Helen pleaded in a high whining voice.

Immediately Zack was at her side. 'Sorry, Mother. If I'd known you would be upset we wouldn't have spoken of it.'

There was a sharp intake of breath from Althea, and Anya knew Helen annoyed her too. Just then Jared caught her eye and smiled, and suddenly she felt warm. She was coming to like Jared Nolan more and more.

'You're up early.'

Anya turned sharply to see Helen

coming towards her. She was wearing a pair of slacks and a sleeveless top, and looking self-conscious about the rightness of them.

'Old habits die hard,' Anya murmured, turning away again. Water was beginning to gush into the pool but it would take ages to fill again.

Helen sat down at the poolside table and began to rustle yesterday's English newspaper. 'Mr. Nolan seems a very nice young man. I was very agreeably surprised.'

Anya was not prepared to discuss him with Helen. 'Is Zack up yet?'

'He had a bad night.' Anya got up slowly and looked at the other woman. 'Althea's going to Cannes today to meet some friends who are staying there, so Zack has decided to rest this morning. He says he'll get some work done this afternoon, which reminds me . . . ' Her eyes were hard as she looked up at Anya. 'I suppose you know that Cèlie wants the afternoon off . . . '

Anya drew a sigh. 'Yes, I know. She

has an important appointment. She mentioned it to me last night.'

'Sit down here with me,' she invited and Anya flopped down dispiritedly into the chair next to Helen's. 'Cèlie is getting a little bit too bold for my liking. She wanted a half hour this morning too. Told me she had a letter that was rather urgent and could she go to the post office. I told her to take it this afternoon on her way out.' Helen eyed Anya curiously. 'Do you think she is seeing Mr. Nolan?'

'How on earth should I know?' And then, regretting her sharpness, added, 'Cèlie doesn't confide in me.'

'Well, I did wonder. You get on well together and you're both the same age, or thereabouts. But she does seem a secretive little thing. A little sly even.'

Anya stared across at the distant hills, deep purple in the morning sun against the cobalt blue of the sky.

'Yes, she is,' Anya answered, aware that for the past two or three days Cèlie hadn't been one of her favourite people either. And then, feeling guilty about such thoughts, added, 'But the children are fond of her, which is important too.'

Her mind was back to yesterday afternoon when she had accompanied Cèlie and the children down to the beach. They'd only been there half an hour when Jared came bounding over the rocks towards them. It was almost as if he had known they would be there, and as it was a last minute decision to go on Anya's part, only Cèlie could have told him. Which made her wonder if something serious was going on between them.

But there was no sign of it in his behaviour. He directed most of his attention towards Jason and Penny, building quite magnificent sand castles for them and devising enough games to keep them occupied all the afternoon. Certainly neither Anya nor Cèlie had cause to feel uncomfortable in his company.

Watching his antics with the two children Anya found herself again being surprised, realising that despite his self-confessed profligate ways he would make an excellent family man.

'You look rather pale, Anya. You're not yourself,' Helen was saying, eyeing her over the top of the newspaper.

Anya managed a smile. 'I'm fine, just a little tired. We *did* get to bed rather late last night.'

Helen laughed. 'Well, it was a pleasant change, I admit, even though I did think Zack was foolish to ask him. It was quite unlike him.' She hesitated and then said, 'As I said I liked Mr. Nolan, but I don't think it's quite the thing for him to be seeing both you and Cèlie.'

She had Anya's full attention again. 'There's no reason why he shouldn't, Helen. He's just a holiday acquaintance as far as I'm concerned.'

The other woman laughed timorously. 'Yes, I suppose so. Someone like Cèlie isn't really the right kind of a girl for a man like Mr. Nolan.'

And me? Anya felt bound to ask, but

diplomatically she remained silent.

'I suspect he comes from a good family. There's breeding there.' Her contemplative eyes came to rest on Anya. 'But, as you say, Anya, holiday friendships are different. It's just a pity Cèlie is asking for more and more free time to be with him and Zack is giving it to her. It's the only way to keep staff these days, I know. It's as well you enjoy looking after the children, dear, and your nursing experience is valuable. You've been quite an asset this year.'

Anya smiled quite genuinely now, knowing that Helen was totally unaware of the insult she had just uttered.

'I'll take them down to the beach. They can play and make as much noise as they want to down there.'

Sylvie, Gervase's wife, came on to the patio carrying a tray. Helen hurriedly folded her newspaper, saying, 'Good, here's my coffee. Care to join me, Anya?'

Anya was already on her feet. 'Not just now, thank you, Helen. I think I'll go inside for a while. I haven't written to Aunt Anna for a week or so. She'll be worried.'

Sylvie put the tray down on the table and, after being thanked by Helen, hurried back into the villa.

'She'll miss you.'

'She misses us all,' Anya answered, 'but every mother hen knows her chicks must leave the nest some time.'

If Helen was aware of any undertone to Anya's voice, or a hidden meaning, she didn't show it. She just poured the steaming coffee into the cup, sighed and said, 'It was just a day like this that Marika died.'

Anya was already past her, going back towards the villa, but she stopped in her tracks, stiffening slightly. 'What makes you mention it now?'

'Just the day, Anya. A little bit breezy, clouds in the sky.' She looked up. The fronds of a palm tree were beginning to wave frantically in the freshening breeze. 'I shouldn't be surprised if there isn't a storm later. I didn't think she would go down to the beach after I'd warned her not to. She just took no notice. I'll never understand why.'

For once Anya felt genuinely sorry for Zack's mother. Tentatively she put one hand on Helen's shoulder. 'You did what you could. You weren't to know she'd take no notice.'

'I think about it quite a lot, you know.'

'You shouldn't. It doesn't help.'

'No,' she said more briskly, raising her cup, 'it doesn't. There's nothing in the world that can help.'

* * *

Anya could hear Cèlie's deeply-accented voice the moment she entered the villa. It came from the playroom down the corridor from the salon. Anya peeped inside and saw the girl sitting on the floor reading a story to the two enraptured children.

Cèlie's hair fell in a dark curtain at either side of her face. Even as she read the story her lips were curved into that secretive, all-knowing smile. Before any of them became aware of her presence Anya hurried away and up the stairs.

She paused outside Zack's door and then knocked quickly, almost at once turning away, but a summons from within arrested her. When she went inside he was standing with his back to the window, still wearing a blue silk dressing-gown over pyjamas of a lighter shade.

His eyes were very dark today, his complexion too. He seemed tense and when he saw that his visitor was Anya his face broke into a semblance of a smile.

'Oh, so it's you, Sweetie.'

'Were you expecting someone else?'

He laughed shortly. 'No, I wasn't expecting anyone.'

He did look ill. She wished he wouldn't work so hard, but forbore to say so.

'How are you feeling, Zack? Your mother said you hadn't slept very well.'

'I woke up with one hell of a headache,' he answered, putting one hand to his head as if to illustrate the point.

'Can I get you anything?'

He smiled, again half-heartedly. 'I've taken some aspirins. It'll go off and perhaps I'll be able to get some sleep.'

'It's my fault. I shouldn't have let you invite Jared round last night. You never entertain while you're writing.'

He shook his head. 'No, it's nothing to do with that. As a matter of fact it made a nice change from a roomful of women.'

'I always thought you liked it that way, Zack,' she said mischievously, 'No competition.'

He smiled in something like his old way. 'I'm hoping there is no competition.' He hesitated, eyeing her carefully. 'I can't say I liked your boyfriend, Sweetie. Too smooth and sure of himself by far.'

Anya stiffened. 'He's not my boyfriend, Zack, and well you know it. And don't say I didn't warn you. I knew you two were oil and water.' She backed towards the door a step or two. 'Are you sure there's nothing troubling you?'

He half turned away and shrugged slightly. 'Come to a bit of a hump, Anya. You know how it is. It happens quite often while I'm working on a manuscript. It'll work out. I'll get down to its this afternoon.' He glanced at her and smiled. 'I'll put the 'Do not disturb' notice on the door.'

She watched him worriedly. 'I think you're working too hard.'

'You may be right,' he answered, 'but I have to go on and do it. *You* understand, Anya, don't you?'

'Yes, I understand,' she whispered.

He suddenly looked brighter. 'Next week, when Althea has her day off, you, me and the children will go out for the day — the whole day! We'll take a picnic lunch and not come back until dark. How about that, Anya? What do you say?'

He looked at her so eagerly she

couldn't help but respond in the same spirit. 'That sounds marvellous, Zack.' Her smile faded then. 'But what about Helen? We can't just leave her here on her own.'

Zack sighed and moved away. 'She hasn't any friends of her own here. She used to have lots before I was a successful writer, but then she drifted away from them. She hasn't been able to make any new ones. The way we live it's difficult . . . '

'I know that, Zack, but you do see how it's going to be for you, always.'

He sighed again and laid his head against the window pane. 'She's my mother. Helen has been a widow a long time. I can't remember my father. Sometimes it was hard for her to keep up appearances. I'm all she has. She can't help being possessive.'

Anya looked at him with pity, for the first time seeing the weary man behind the elegant, gay façade she had loved for so long. She had never thought to pity Zack.

'I'm not possessive,' she said softly.

'Every woman is without knowing it.' He walked over to the dresser and poured a measure of whisky from a selection of drinks he always kept in his room. 'Want one?' he asked.

She shook her head. 'Not this time of the morning.'

The room was the one he had shared with Marika. It still bore her personality quite forcibly. Done out in different shades of pink and ivory it was hardly a man's room, and yet Zack did not look out of place in it.

'I suppose you know Jason will be going to school in September.'

'Yes.'

He looked at her. 'Will you see to it for me, Anya? Otherwise . . . Mother loves them, but, well, you know, Anya . . . '

It was her turn to sigh. 'Yes, I know. You don't have to worry, Zack. I told you the other day I'll take care of them, and that means wherever they go. The welfare of Jason and Penny will always be important to me. I'll take them to London in September. You won't have to worry about finding someone else to look after them.'

'I'm very grateful.'

'You don't have to be,' she told him and her mouth was suddenly dry. She pulled open the door. 'You'd better rest now.' And then, closing the door as she went out, she added, 'I'll see you later.'

She closed the door with a loud snap and stood with her back against it for a moment or two. She had never seen Zack so nervy or depressed before and it came as a shock to her to see him vulnerable. After a while she roused herself and went to her own room. She supposed anyone with an artistic talent as great as Zack's must expect such moods of despondency from time to time. It still troubled her though.

7

A thick layer of grey raincloud obscured the sky and rain dripped down the windowpane with monotonous regularity.

Anya stood at the playroom window, staring out, her arms folded on the windowledge in front of her. Behind her Jason frowned thoughtfully as he created a picture and Penny circled round the spacious room on her tricycle.

It had been quite some time since, at the first ominous sign of rain, she had bundled the children and their toys up the steps and back into the villa, beating the downpour by only a minute or two. Now she was feeling vaguely resentful and not for anything would she admit to herself it was because Jared hadn't joined them today. Not that she really expected him to. She had seen Cèlie leaving after lunch, dressed in her best clothes. She had been wearing a new suit which looked remarkably chic. It gave Anya something of a jolt to realise it must have cost quite a lot of money, and as far as she was concerned a woman only dressed like that when she was meeting a man.

The door opened and Anya turned round, expecting to see Cèlie at last, her face flushed and her lips curved into a smile. But it was Helen, looking a little breathless and slightly windswept.

'What terrible weather,' she gasped, 'and this is only the beginning. I almost got drenched to the skin just coming from the garage to the house. Whoever designed this villa must have been mad to put the garage so far from the house.'

The children went on playing as if their grandmother was not there, which served as an indication of the extent of their affection for her. Anya's heart warmed to think of how they always rushed to greet her whatever else they were doing.

'I expect the idea was to save being disturbed by vehicles coming and going. I must admit I never hear any cars and I like that. When I lived at the nurse's home ambulances and cars passed my bedroom window at all hours of the day and night.'

Jason held up his painting for his grandmother to see.

'That's very nice, dear, very nice indeed,' she murmured and then looked at Anya again. 'I've just peeped in on Zack. He's feeling very much better and he's still hard at work, but I've managed to persuade him to stop for some tea.' She shook her head. 'He still looks positively hollow-eyed.'

Penny had abandoned her tricycle and was pulling at Anya's hand, whimpering a little.

'Hasn't Cèlie come back yet?' Helen asked.

Anya shook her head despondently. 'She was due back about an hour ago.'

'She's probably sheltering. It really is very nasty out. I knew it would turn out like this today and if I hadn't needed so much shopping I wouldn't have ventured out at all.'

Anya looked down at her niece and smiled. 'It's their tea time. I'll take them down to Sylvie and if Cèlie hasn't come back by the time they've eaten I'll play with them until bedtime.'

Cèlie still hadn't returned quite late in the evening and it fell to Anya to bathe the children and put them to bed, even though they asked for Cèlie. Anya had kept them up later in case she returned.

'You would think she would telephone after all this time to make her excuses!' Helen cried in indignation over dinner.

'She may not be near one,' Zack pointed out, and then, smiling faintly, 'Even if she were, she might not think of it.' He brandished his fork dramatically in the air. 'Depend on it, we won't see her until tomorrow. If she's with one of her boyfriends she'll be only too pleased of an excuse to stay out for the night.'

'I always thought she was a tramp,' Helen answered contemptuously.

Anya couldn't say anything at all.

She slept in the nursery that night and when she awoke the sky was still a leaden grey, but the wind had dropped a little and the rain had all but stopped. This morning the children were too excited at the novelty of having Auntie Anya sleeping in the nursery to question where Cèlie was. How quickly they forget, she thought sadly.

She left them having breakfast and went down to join the others in the dining-room. They were already present, talking quietly amongst themselves, and eating from the various breakfast dishes. Not for them the spartan continental breakfast.

Anya was relieved to see Zack smiling and back to his old jovial frame of mind. The play must be going well again.

'Any word from Cèlie?' she asked breathlessly.

'None at all,' answered Zack.

'I don't think we'll see her again,' Althea murmured. She hadn't come back until very late last night. It was well after midnight when Anya had finally fallen asleep and Althea hadn't returned by then. 'If you ask me, she's eloped.'

'She might have had an accident,' Anya suggested, buttering a roll half-heartedly.

'We'd have heard by now,' answered Helen, drawing a sigh. 'You just can't rely on anyone these days.'

'She's been missing all night,' Anya insisted, and then, turning to Zack, 'Don't you think we should contact the police?'

Zack laughed and filled her cup with coffee. 'Police! Cèlie won't thank us for doing that, Sweetie, not if she's doing what we think she's doing.'

'You're only supposing she's with a man,' Anya snapped.

Althea smiled and popped a piece of toast into her mouth. 'I think Anya's upset at the thought of *which* man Cèlie is with.'

Anya cast her a furious look and Zack said, 'I don't believe Jared Nolan means anything to Anya. Does he, Sweetie?'

'Of course not.'

Althea shrugged. 'I thought he was rather attractive.'

'I don't pay you to find other men attractive,' Zack quipped.

'I don't know how you can joke about it,' Anya protested. 'I can't help feeling, whatever you say, that Cèlie just wouldn't go off without telling us!'

Althea finished her coffee and got to her feet. 'It's all very tiresome, I can tell you. I'm certainly not going to let it trouble me.'

'Anya can't help herself,' Zack explained. 'She's the worrying kind. Aren't you, Sweetie?' He pinched her cheek and she twisted away from him.

Althea walked towards the door. 'I'm

too busy to worry. You must have worked like a demon yesterday to do so much in one afternoon. It's going to take me two days to type it up.'

'I did work hard,' he admitted, glancing worriedly at Anya as his secretary left the room.

Helen was crumbling a roll nervously onto her plate until it was filled with crumbs. 'I couldn't bear the thought of having the police in.'

Zack poured another cup of coffee for himself whilst Anya's remained untouched. 'The police aren't going to be called in. We'll probably get a telegram from her telling us she's with the most marvellous man and she's not coming back. It happens all the time. I remember it happened to Austin Kerr last year when they took a villa in Malta. And he has four children! The wretched girl took two weeks to let them know where she was — in Istanbul of all places! — and then only because she wanted her clothes sending on.'

He glanced at Anya as he gulped at the coffee. 'Come on, Sweetie, drink up.' Anya obeyed automatically. 'How are you managing with Jason and Penny? They're not proving too much for you, are they?'

Anya smiled faintly. 'Of course not, Zack. I have help anyway now. One of the girls who helps Sylvie with the heavy work — Rose — is looking after them at the moment. She comes from a large family herself and she has endless patience. She hasn't been married long herself — to one of the St. Brilac fishermen — and she's only too pleased to look after them. She's agreed to help me with Jason and Penny until . . . ' She looked away, ' . . . until Cèlie comes back.'

Zack pushed his chair back and stood up, dabbing at his lips with the linen serviette as he did so. 'That's splendid, but I'll tell you something, Anya, if that little tramp does come back now she'll get her marching orders.'

His lips were clamped into a tight

line. 'But we don't know . . . ' Anya began to protest, but it was no use. He had already gone.

Anya was in the hall. She could hear Helen's voice berating, in appalling French, some hapless tradesman over the telephone. She shrugged into a light raincoat and covered her hair with a scarf. As she passed the open door to the salon she saw Helen pause and put her hand over the mouthpiece as if about to say something to her, but she hurried on, past Zack's study and the little office next to it where Althea could be heard busily typing.

Anya hurried through the garden and down the steps, which, after the storm, were treacherously slippery. The sand, too, was damp and clammy to her feet and it seemed to take her a long time to cross the beach, and then she ran as fast as she could through the wood, over damp pine needles which silenced her progress, and beneath dripping branches. She had no wish to loiter today in this dark secretive place. She never would again.

By the time she reached St. Brilac the breeze had dropped even more. It had dispersed the clouds and the sun was pushing its way through. It was reflected dully in the puddles on the quay.

Anya looked anxiously for the *Sea Urchin* and her heart leapt involuntarily when she caught sight of it in its berth, and then again when she saw Jared at the *Bar Americaine*. He was smiling unconcernedly as he stood, leaning with one hand on a chair as he talked to Jules who was wiping the rain off the plastic covered chairs and mopping up the little pools that had collected on the tables.

'Jared!' She began to run towards him. He turned and there was a smile on his face which widened when he saw her. A smile of genuine pleasure, she was sure. She was suddenly so glad to see him.

'Anya, how nice to see you! I was going to call at the villa later this morning and now you've saved me the walk.'

'Can I talk to you?' she asked breathlessly.

His smile faded and his eyes searched her face. 'Of course you can.'

She smiled a belated greeting to Jules and said, 'Shall we go inside?'

'*Deaux café au lait*, Jules, *s'il vous plait*,' he ordered as he followed her into the bar.

'*Certainement, monsieur*,' the man replied.

Jared ushered her to a table in the corner of the room. At this time of the day there were few people in the bar anyway. Anya pulled off her scarf as she sat down and unfastened her raincoat. Now she had found him she was feeling a little self-conscious. Perhaps Althea and Zack were right; she was worrying unnecessarily.

As he sat down next to her his eyes were questioning. 'You want to talk,' he reminded her.

'Were you with Cèlie yesterday

afternoon?' she asked quickly so that it was over.

He displayed little surprise and after a slight hesitation answered. 'No, I didn't see her at all yesterday. Should I have done?'

'Cèlie went out yesterday after lunch. I thought she might have been with you.'

'No, not me, but if you're so interested in who she was with, why don't you ask her?'

He was looking amused now. Did he really think she would care if he'd been with Cèlie if the girl had come back?

Jules came over with their coffee and put them down on the table. 'You don't understand,' she said hoarsely as Jules withdrew, 'Cèlie didn't come back last night.'

He had been in the process of tearing open a sachet of sugar, but now he stopped and put it down. 'She's missing?'

Anya nodded. He went on putting the sugar into his coffee. 'I wasn't the only man around here who was seeing her.'

'You were the only man I *knew*.'

'I'm sorry, I can't help you,' he answered, staring thoughtfully into his cup. 'I met her here once and we talked about her life and I invited her out so we could talk about opportunities in Canada. That's all.'

Anya looked at him disbelievingly. 'And did you talk about Canada?'

He sipped slowly at his coffee. Anya roused herself, sweetened hers and began to drink it.

'No, not really. She didn't seem interested the second time. She said she thought she would stay nearer home. Perhaps there was a man in her life; an *affaire* that turned serious.'

'I can't believe a man of the world could fall for such a tale in the first place,' she scoffed.

He looked at her in surprise. 'A female cynic, heaven help us. What's given *you* the idea that I'm a sex fiend?'

Anya blushed and looked away. 'I'm

not Cèlie, am I?'

He made a great show of looking her up and down. 'Perhaps you don't possess as much as Cèlie,' he said at last, 'but it's all in the right place. You're certainly no less of a woman.'

'Thanks, but we were talking about Cèlie.'

He leaned forward. 'I got the impression that she was enjoying her job; enjoying it very much indeed. I don't think she'd stay away without good reason.'

'Neither do I.'

He examined his nails thoughtfully. 'Have you suggested calling in the police?'

'They won't hear of it. Zack, Althea and Helen all think she's with a man somewhere and if we call in the police we'll be making laughing stocks of ourselves.'

'And I suppose I was the man?' She didn't answer. 'They're probably right — about it being a man, I mean. Cèlie didn't flaunt herself but you and I know she's a sexy little number.'

'You may know, Jared,' she answered demurely, 'but I certainly have no reason to.'

He gave a little laugh. 'Puritanical little devil, aren't you? Well, you won't find Cèlie's knickers in my bunk. One good night kiss and that was the end of it. I felt more like her brother.'

'Oh brother!' Anya groaned. 'I'd better get back before they post me missing too.'

As she stood up to go she found him towering over her. 'Your brother-in-law is probably right when he said she'd gone with a man, Anya . . . '

'But so suddenly?'

'It does sometimes happen like that — a sudden wanting never to be apart again. Not everyone is as conscientious as you about responsibilities.'

She couldn't meet his gaze. 'Come on,' he said briskly, 'I'll walk you back to the villa. I still don't like you to walk through the wood alone.'

They were passing through the door

to the outside. Jared raised his hand to wave goodbye to Jules when Anya gripped his other hand tightly.

He looked down at her, his eyes serious for once. 'You don't think something awful has happened to her, do you, Jared?'

She had voiced her unspoken fear at last, her eyes were wide with apprehension, but he made no reply to comfort her.

8

Lunch was a miserable meal, not only for Anya, but seemingly so for the others too. The meal proceeded with general small talk which soon faded away when a mood of depression descended on them all. Anya wished she had stayed with the children. At least their continual chatter was diverting.

No one had a particularly hearty appetite; they all toyed with their food, making a pretence of eating until Zack pushed away his plate, saying, 'Drat that girl. If we don't hear from her soon I'll *have* to inform the police.'

Anya sighed with relief. The police would soon find her. It would be far better than this awful waiting and continual conjecture.

'Perhaps it would be best,' murmured Althea. 'It is most thoughtless of her, I must admit.'

'Do we have to?' moaned Helen, who had dropped her fork the moment the police were mentioned. 'They'll be all over the place, asking questions, prying into our most private business.'

No one answered her, but Anya said, in a subdued voice that could hardly be heard, 'I still believe Cèlie would have got in touch with us if she could.'

'Oh, some girls are completely thoughtless,' Althea answered, dismissing the matter airily, 'but we must know what she is doing — for our own convenience.'

Anya shot her an angry glance; nothing had yet interfered with any of Althea's plans. Anya still felt a heavy dread inside her and when she looked at Zack's face, his brow creased, she knew he was worried too, and she was even more frightened.

He stood up slowly. 'Well, I shan't contact the police just yet. You never know . . . '

He had eaten practically nothing, which Anya knew was a bad sign in

Zack. She realised now that he was far more worried than he wanted to admit.

When Sylvie came hurrying in he said in a weary voice, 'You may as well clear away now, Sylvie. None of us are very hungry.'

'*Oui, monsieur.*' She remained where she was, glancing round at each glum face. 'There is a gentleman waiting to see you, monsieur — a policeman.'

They were all alert. Zack rushed out of the dining room like a greyhound out of its trap, and the others were scarcely far behind. A plain-clothes policeman and a uniformed *agent* were waiting in the salon.

'Inspector Sandray, monsieur,' he introduced himself. He was a drab little man, balding, but his eyes were bright.

Anya guessed he would be shrewd. Those eyes would miss very little.

'I assume you have news of my employee, Mademoiselle Danielle . . . ' Zack said breathlessly.

'Bad news, I'm afraid, monsieur. I regret to inform you that Mademoiselle

154

Danielle is dead.'

Helen let out an agonised cry and crumpled into a chair. Anya, despite her fears, felt his words like a blow and covered her trembling lips with her hand. Althea looked as if she had been turned to stone, and Zack simply slumped unseeingly into an armchair.

Anya made a conscious effort to control the hysteria that was welling up inside her and went hurriedly to Helen who was crying heartbrokenly into her hands. She wondered why. Cèlie had meant less than nothing to Helen.

'How?' whispered Zack.

'She was strangled,' the Inspector answered. His own voice was emotionless. He had broken such news countless times before. 'There will be many questions you wish to ask me, and I have some of my own, but perhaps first *madame* would like some brandy.'

'That's a very good idea,' said Anya, fighting back her own tears.

'I'll get it,' Althea offered, rousing herself out of her own stupor at last. 'One for you too, Anya?'

Anya shook her head and then looked at the inspector. The *agent* remained by the door, silent and anonymous. 'I think she should be taken to her room.'

'All in good time, mam'selle, but for now I would prefer her to remain here. I will detain you all no longer than necessary.'

Althea handed Helen a glass of brandy and when she didn't take it Anya started to coax her as if she were a baby. Out of the corner of her eye she saw Althea pour more brandy for herself and for Zack. By the time Helen had finished hers she was much recovered.

'It is a very great shock,' murmured the inspector as he sat down in one of the armchairs.

Althea's hand shook so much as she tried to drink that she had to grip the glass with both hands. Zack suddenly jumped to his feet and ran from the room.

'He's going to be sick,' said his mother in a wooden voice. 'He always is when he's upset. On opening night he's just the same.'

'I feel sick myself,' Anya answered.

Althea sank down on to the arm of the sofa. For once her immaculately groomed head, always carried so proudly, drooped dispiritedly. 'I think we all do,' she murmured.

'It's most distressing,' commented the inspector as he drummed with the fingers of one hand on the arm of his chair.

Zack came back in then. He murmured an apology and sank back into the chair. He had the shambling walk of a very old man. His hair was tousled, his face unusually pale.

'Where . . . where did you find her?'

'At a beach not far from St. Raphael. It is a lonely place.'

'Who did it?' His voice was harsh.

The inspector gave a deprecating

157

little smile. 'We do not know that yet. She died some time yesterday afternoon. The rain that followed obliterated many of the clues.'

Zack let out a sigh and laid his head back on the chair, closing his eyes.

'And now,' said Inspector Sandray, taking his notebook and pencil from his pocket, 'if you could answer just a few questions. I will be as brief as possible for now.

'Mademoiselle Danielle worked for you as a children's nurse, I understand . . . '

Inexorably the questions went on and Zack answered them woodenly while the others sat, still suffering to some degree from shock. It was awful, so awful that the fact had hardly registered. Anya supposed the girl's family would have to be informed; she was glad she wasn't the one to do it.

'And now if you would please, monsieur, tell me what your movements were between say 2 p.m. and 5.30 p.m. yesterday.'

'That's a ridiculous question!' cried Helen. 'What have my son's movements to do with this girl's death?'

The inspector half-turned to look at her, smiling apologetically. 'It is just a matter of routine, madame.'

Althea shuddered. 'It's all so horrible, I can't believe it's happened.'

'I was working in my study, Inspector,' Zack answered, 'from about two o'clock until well after seven.'

'And your secretary? She was with you?'

'I was in Cannes with friends all day,' Althea answered. 'I didn't return until about one o'clock this morning. When I returned Mr. Anderson had left a considerable amount of work that he had done during the afternoon.'

The inspector eyed Althea with interest. 'May I have the names of these friends you were with?'

Althea gave a bewildered little laugh. To Anya it sounded as if it were bordering on hysteria. 'Mr. and Mrs. Adrian Coulson. They were staying at the International.'

'Were?'

Althea looked away. 'They left first thing this morning.'

'No doubt they can be contacted to corroborate your story.'

'Really, Inspector, is all this necessary?' Helen asked, having recovered considerably. 'Surely you can't think one of us . . . '

The inspector gave her one of his rare smiles. 'It is necessary to establish the innocence of those involved just as it is necessary to establish the guilt of the murderer. Did you remain here, *madame*, yesterday afternoon?'

Helen looked momentarily taken aback and then answered slowly, 'No, I went to Hyeres to do some shopping. When I returned it was already raining. I went in to see my son.' She looked at Zack. 'It was about six o'clock, I believe . . . '

Zack shook his head. 'When I'm working well I lose all track of time.'

When the inspector turned to Anya

she was ready for him. Her voice when she spoke was thick. 'I was looking after Mr. Anderson's two children — my niece and nephew. We were on the beach until it began to rain and then we came back here. Cèlie — Miss Danielle — was supposed to come back in time to give the children their evening meal.'

The inspector nodded and Anya said impulsively, 'You will find whoever's done this, won't you?'

'We will try, mam'selle; we will certainly try.' He drew a sigh. 'The trouble is, on the Cote d'Azur, there is such a big floating population. The murderer may have left soon after with so many other tourists. Today he may be in Amsterdam, or Paris, or London. Even New York. It is very difficult.' He paused for a moment and then said thoughtfully, 'I was wondering why Miss Danielle's disappearance was not reported to us . . . '

'That was my fault, Inspector,' Zack said quickly. 'It was suggested, but I preferred to wait — in case she had met a friend and was sheltering from the storm.'

'Ah, that is very understandable. Do you know of any friends she may have had?'

Anya looked up sharply. Her throat suddenly became dry. Zack looked alert for the first time since the inspector had arrived.

'There is only Jared Nolan,' he said.

'Zack!'

Anya wasn't quite sure why she felt so shocked, or so frightened when Jared's name was inevitably mentioned. Zack looked perplexed.

'He *has* been seeing her.'

'Only on two occasions,' Anya answered and found every occupant of the room watching her curiously, and she lapsed into an embarrassed silence.

'Actually, we did assume that they were seeing each other yesterday afternoon,' Zack went on, addressing the inspector once more.

'That is most helpful. Where can I find this Jared Nolan?'

'He has a boat moored at St. Brilac.' Zack snapped his fingers. 'What is it called, Anya?'

'*Sea Urchin*,' she answered, feeling slightly sick.

'Did she speak of any other friends?' the inspector asked the room at large.

The others shook their heads. Anya said, 'She told me she had made many friends in St. Brilac.'

The others looked disbelieving. If the circumstances had been different they would have looked amused. The inspector remained expressionless and said, 'Did she mention any by name?'

Anya shook her head and the inspector snapped the notebook shut with the air of a man who had solved the case. Anya felt as if she could hit Zack. Nothing could be gained by involving Jared in this sordid mess.

'Now I should like to speak to the staff for a few moments,' said Inspector Sandray, getting to his feet. 'Then, monsieur,' he added looking at Zack, 'I should be glad if you would accompany me . . . '

Anya and Althea gasped. Helen let out a cry, but before anyone could say anything the inspector explained, 'It would be helpful to us if Monsieur Anderson could make the formal identification. It is merely a formality but it would help us a great deal.'

Zack looked sick again. Anya knew he had no stomach for such a task, but he nodded, saying, 'Of course, Inspector. Anything to help.' He hesitated and then asked, 'Any idea why, Inspector?'

The man looked vague. 'Possibly robbery. The contents of her handbag were scattered about. But it is too soon to say for sure . . . '

Helen escorted the two policemen out of the room and Althea let out a deep sigh. 'What a sorry mess.' She chafed her arms absently. 'Trust that stupid girl to get herself killed.'

Anya was still furious at Zack and some of that fury spilled over as she retorted, 'I'm sure she didn't do it deliberately, Althea. Young, attractive women with life in front of them don't usually have themselves killed on purpose.'

'It won't help if we start squabbling,' Zack pointed out, his voice flat and devoid of all expression.

'It won't help bringing Jared Nolan's name into it either!' He looked up sharply, his dark eyes were filled with genuine bewilderment. 'It was unnecessary, Zack.'

'I don't agree,' Althea broke in. 'I think Zack was perfectly right. Jared Nolan probably knew her a great deal better than any of us.'

'That's just where you're wrong. He didn't! He only saw her twice.'

'He was probably with her yesterday,' Zack pointed out.

'He wasn't.'

Both Zack and Althea looked at her curiously. 'How do you know, Anya? You were here all day yourself, weren't you?'

Much of Anya's anger evaporated.

'Yes, I was, but Jared told me he only knew Cèlie slightly.' They both continued to look at her. 'I spoke to him this morning.'

'Oh, did you?' murmured Zack, looking vaguely vexed and more than a little thoughtful.

'Well, someone had to do something. I thought I'd ask around, see if anyone had seen Cèlie.'

'And he said he hadn't,' Althea put in.

Anya didn't answer but Zack said, 'He's hardly likely to admit to it, is he?'

'You're talking as if he's guilty!'

Zack got to his feet. He looked nothing like the suave and handsome man of years gone by.

'I don't know about that, Anya, but if the inspector feels bound to ask *us* our movements yesterday, then I reckon Nolan is entitled to answer a few questions too.'

Anya gave a gasp of exasperation as he went out of the room. Althea stood up and went across to the drinks trolley again. 'You really need a strong drink,' she said to Anya.

'No, thank you, but go ahead, have one yourself.'

Althea poured herself another generous measure of brandy and then she began to prowl the room. Anya had laid her head back on the sofa, her mind full of the horror of the last half hour. In her heart she knew that, possibly, more unpleasantness was to come.

'When something like this happens,' Anya mused, 'it makes me wonder if I could have done something to stop it.' Althea stopped to look at her. 'If I'd taken more notice of her. Perhaps if I'd invited her confidence.'

'That's ridiculous,' Althea answered, going over to the window. 'That's useless conjecture. That girl wouldn't have confided in her own priest.'

'I suppose you're right,' Anya sighed.

'I must say I was surprised at how fiercely you defended Jared Nolan. Zack had no right to withhold his name. He had no reason to.'

'I suppose not.'

'Really, Jared Nolan is the number one suspect.' Anya flashed her a furious look. 'How many men could Cèlie have been seeing after all? She hadn't been here that long and she didn't have so much free time.'

'I believe he's innocent.'

'You're an innocent yourself,' she said, smiling slightly. 'Anyway, the police will soon find out if he's guilty or not, so it needn't trouble us unduly.'

Anya gave an involuntary little shudder and Althea went on, 'Actually this could be a stroke of luck for you, this girl's unfortunate death.'

Anya sat up straight, her eyes wide. 'What do you mean, Althea?'

The older girl smiled again as she sat down unhurriedly at the far side of the sofa. 'You've been wanting a stronger hold on Zack ever since your sister died. Now you can take charge of the children. What better hold can there be? You certainly didn't fool me with your pretended infatuation with Jared Nolan.

I am quite aware Zack is the only one you're infatuated with.'

'I don't like what you're inferring, Althea. It's totally unfair and totally untrue.'

'But it is true,' she answered complacently, finishing off her brandy and allowing the glass to drop negligently through her fingers to the floor. 'It was already arranged for me to take charge of the children when Cèlie left in September.'

'And then?' Anya looked away. 'We may as well be honest, Anya, you don't want to remain the children's nanny until they're grown up. You want Zack.'

'That's up to Zack himself.'

'You're not suited to him, Anya. Surely you can see that for yourself?' Anya said nothing. 'You haven't got the qualities necessary for the job.'

'And I suppose you have,' Anya shot at her.

'Yes, I have. I know all his moods, and I know how to treat him at all times. I understand his work as no other person can. It takes more than a dreamy kind of worship to make the right partner for him.' Anya's hands clenched into fists at her side. In the hall she could hear the inspector's voice.

'You've got to know how to give with Zack,' Althea was saying softly. 'He'd never send his mother away. She'd always be there. I could cope with that, Anya.' She looked at her. 'Could you?'

Anya swallowed convulsively. 'Marika coped.'

'Yes, she did, and often by burying her own feelings. You'd have to learn to be more controlled, and really, Anya, I don't think you could. Zack is a very talented person. He's special. He has to be treated as such. You really don't stand much of a chance against me. I know him too well.'

Anya jumped to her feet. 'This is the most ridiculous conversation. This doesn't call for the judgement of Solomon, Althea. Zack will make up his

170

own mind. We're not two dogs with one bone.'

'Zack is a man who needs the right kind of woman in the background. I think his mind can be made up for him.' Althea's eyes passed coldly over her. She didn't seem daunted that Anya for once towered over her. 'You'd face a far better future going back to London, having lots of boyfriends until you meet the one you want to marry. You're still very much the child and Zack needs a mature woman. You know very well Zack can always get someone to look after the children for him. It would save you an awful lot of heartache.'

Anya's whole body shook with fury, or perhaps it was just delayed shock. She couldn't be sure. She just felt shattered.

'You're a cool one,' she said, her voice hardly above a whisper.

Althea pulled her skirt down over her knee and then she looked up artlessly. 'Haven't I been telling you that?'

Anya turned away and then abruptly

moved towards the patio doors. 'I'm going out. I must go out.'

She fumbled with the sliding doors, opening them just enough to slip through. She hurried away from the villa and then paused to glance back. Althea was pouring out another tumblerful of brandy. She no longer looked shocked or upset. She looked rather pleased with herself.

9

The return of fine weather ensured that the quay was crowded with people. Boats bobbed up and down in the water and many of the berths were empty. Anya had run all the way from the villa as if some unseen devil were chasing her. It was worse than that. It was just as if a beautiful stained-glass window had shattered to fragments before her eyes.

Her eyes strained to see if *Sea Urchin* was in its berth. Dread weighed heavily inside her for fear that it was not there. And then she saw the boat, unmistakable with its bright blue and white paintwork. No one was on deck. Anya hesitated, glancing across at the *Bar Americaine*, unable to decide whether to call there first or not.

After a moment or two, although her breath was coming in heavy, uneven gasps, she ran towards the boat, pushing her way impatiently through the throng.

As she jumped on board she called his name. 'Jared. Jared! Are you there?'

Immediately the hatch flew open and to her relief he stepped on to the deck. He stopped dead when he saw her, his face registering a number of emotions in a matter of seconds. Anya knew that her own emotions were very clear; her verbal exchange with Althea, coming so soon after the news about Cèlie, had been the breaking point.

'Oh Jared!' she cried and, rushing forward into his arms, she began to cry heartbrokenly.

He didn't question her or say anything at all for a minute or two while he held her as sobs racked her body. Then when she was a little calmer and she lifted her head from the comfort of his shoulder to look at him, he asked, 'Cèlie?'

She nodded. His face was set into an expression of extreme grimness. 'What happened to her?'

'Someone . . . strangled her,' she gasped, pulling away from him at last, wiping her damp cheeks with the handkerchief she had hastily fumbled for.

He let out a long breath. 'Good God.'

Anya choked back another sob and allowed him to lead her into the cabin. When she was seated on the bunk he handed her a glass of water but she brushed it aside.

'There must have been some way of avoiding that,' he said through his teeth.

She looked up at him with eyes still awash with tears. 'Do you feel like that too?'

He nodded and sank down on to the bunk opposite. 'Heaven only knows how it could have been stopped but I can't help feeling there was something, if I'd tried hard enough.'

'Me too. But Althea says it's foolish feeling like that.'

He roused himself slightly, saying,

'It's just as well we're not all carved from ice.'

Anya gave a harsh little laugh, glad in a small way that Jared had not been charmed by Althea or impressed by her cold beauty.

He looked at her worriedly then. 'Are you all right, Anya?'

She nodded and smiled half-heartedly. 'It was good to get it out of my system. I'd been holding it in since we had the news. I knew all along something had happened to her.'

'Possibly they all did — me too. No one likes to voice that kind of suspicion. We're all optimists by nature.' He hesitated. 'Have the police been to question you?'

'Yes, the inspector was very nice and reassuring.' She shuddered. 'But I'm sure he missed nothing.' She raised her eyes slowly to meet his. 'Jared, Zack told him you'd been seeing Cèlie.'

He shrugged slightly. 'So I had. We'll all have to answer questions, I suppose.'

'Where were you yesterday?' she

asked, suddenly with urgency. She had to know.

'Here,' he said, evidently surprised by her question.

'In St. Brilac? Around the village?'

'No, on the boat. I took it out to sea in the morning.

Thought I'd do some fishing. I enjoy it from time to time. The infinity of the sea all around me has the effect of clearing the mind, making it more receptive.'

Anya watched him steadily. 'Were you alone?'

'No! I had half a dozen nubile young women on board with me! I like them in multiples of two, you see. It's rather like aspirins — you take two every four hours.'

Anya jumped to her feet. 'Oh, Jared, don't joke about it. It's serious. You have no alibi.'

'I shouldn't think I'll need one.'

She twisted her handkerchief around her hand in anguish. 'But you do. Everyone at the villa can account for their time. Cèlie wouldn't have known many people here and yet she went to meet someone she did know, and it's likely that person . . . killed her.'

His face became a wooden mask. 'It wasn't me.'

'Zack and Althea both think you . . . did it,' she said quickly. 'The police might think so too.'

'Don't worry, Anya. No one is going to accuse me of something I didn't do.'

'But they might! It would be so easy.'

'And the motive?'

She swallowed noisily and shrugged half-heartedly. 'They'd soon find one. They could say you'd tried to make love to her and she'd refused . . . or something like that.'

'Yes, and they could say I'd been trying to rob the casino at Cannes.' He got to his feet and put both hands on her shoulders, looking into her fear-filled eyes. 'You're really getting yourself into a state for nothing, you know. The police are just as likely to arrest your brother-in-law. Why aren't you quaking with fear for him?'

For a moment she was stunned into silence as she searched her mind for an answer. At last she said, 'He was in his study all afternoon.'

'The police,' he said gently, 'don't just compile a list of suspects and put a pin in the paper to decide which one did it.'

'Jared, a girl died here last year. Remember? We talked about it.'

His face looked suddenly grim. 'I remember. What about it?'

'The police never found the murderer. They won't like to fail again. It wouldn't be good for their image, and they might just go for the most obvious one . . .'

He smiled. 'And who says that I am the most obvious suspect? I had no idea I looked as if I might have criminal tendencies.'

She looked up at him appealingly. 'Won't you take this seriously?'

'Anya, having seen the law at work so many times, I have a profound respect for it. You have no need to fear for me. Only promise me you won't go rushing around on your own until this matter is cleared up.'

She sighed and nodded, moving away from him. 'I had to come. Inspector Sandray will be coming to question you.'

'I'll be ready.'

She moved out on to the deck and he followed her. Gulls wheeled and screamed overhead. She took a deep lungful of sweet, sea air, turning to look at the white buildings clustering up the cliff.

'I know you're going to think this is a proposition,' he ventured, and she looked at him again, 'but would you like to sleep here tonight? I can beg a room from Jules. He'll fix one up for me.'

'Why on earth should I do that?'

'The atmosphere at the villa can't be very cheerful just now. You might feel happier away from there. I mean it, Anya, I'd be glad if you did.'

She smiled, grateful for his concern,

but she shook her head. 'I wouldn't dream of leaving the villa just at the moment. I want to know just what is going on in the investigation. Besides, I must help with the children.'

Jared's face suddenly contorted with bitterness. 'He really has a hold over you with those children, hasn't he?'

She stiffened. 'That's not a very diplomatic way of putting it. Perhaps, as Althea has already pointed out, it's me who has the hold over Zack through the children.'

'What a charming crowd you're associated with.'

'I'd better get back.'

'I'll come with you,' he said, reaching for a sweater and then closing the hatch. She was about to protest when he added, 'As far as the beach anyway. I don't suppose I'll be welcome at the villa today.'

Anya climbed on to the quay and he was about to follow when he stopped and looked at her, one foot on the deck and one foot on the quay. As she looked at him, standing there, so tall and so straight, her throat constricted as she felt an unfamiliar emotion. She looked away from him quickly, trying to still the frantic beating of her heart.

'Anya, how can you be so sure it isn't me?'

For a moment she didn't realise what he meant and then her eyes opened wide in alarm.

'I know, Jared. I just know.'

*   *   *

Despite her determination to return to the villa, Anya dreaded it, but when she approached the pool she was surprised first of all to see Helen wearing a gay sundress and stretched out on a beach bed, and Althea reading a story to Jason and Penny who were listening to her with rapt attention.

Anya hesitated on the edge of the patio and Althea looked up and paused to smile, then she continued reading aloud. The scene before her was so normal, so ordinary, that Anya shuddered involuntarily. It was just like a normal day except that Althea was not working; Cèlie might not be lying dead on a cold marble slab.

Just then Anya had a strange yearning to be back with Jared; she needed his sense of humour and that rock hard dependability she could sense in him. But she had come back.

'Is Zack back yet?' she asked in an uneven voice. Zack was the one person she had no wish to see just then.

His mother sat up and removed her sunglasses. 'He came back about fifteen minutes ago. Poor lamb, he looked as white as a ghost. He's gone upstairs to rest. He says he won't be down again tonight. This sort of thing affects him terribly. He's so sensitive.'

Anya sank down on the edge of one of the beach beds and stared into the pool. 'I don't think I could eat anything myself tonight.'

'The inspector searched Cèlie's room before he left. Oh, and all those questions he asked. It makes one feel there is no privacy left at all.'

'It's his job. It shouldn't matter to the innocent.'

Helen's eyes studied the dejected figure sitting next to her. 'You shouldn't have gone out this afternoon, Anya.'

She looked up at last. The pool was beginning to dazzle her. 'Did the police want me?'

'No,' she answered in surprise. 'I just thought it inadvisable for you to be seeing that young man until this unpleasant business is cleared up.'

'Nonsense,' she answered shortly. 'Jared has had nothing to do with it. I'd stake my life on that.'

'That's exactly what you may have done, dear, every time you've seen him.'

Anya made a sound of impatience and then Helen said, lowering her voice considerably, 'I'm glad to have this opportunity of talking to you alone. Zack has asked Althea to write to some estate agents in London.' Anya's interest quickened. 'He wants to buy a house in the country where the children and I can live for part of the year. It will be a settled home for them.'

Anya looked at her in dismay now. 'But Zack asked me . . . '

'To look after them? Yes, I know, dear, but he realises now it isn't fair to you. So young. No, it's for me to make a home for them and I intend to do it. We'll come here in the summer, of course, as always, but with all this unpleasantness, the business of buying a house away from here is more acute now.'

'But I *want* to look after them, Helen.'

She put one hand on Anya's arm. Her nails were painted with bright red enamel. The sight of it repulsed Anya; they looked as if they were stained with blood.

'Your intentions are so good,' she said, 'but if you think about it, not very practical. You are young and you have a life of your own to lead. They are, after all, my grandchildren, and my son is a widower. It's what any mother would do. And, of course, you, dear, can visit us whenever you wish, but I expect for most of the time you'll have your own life to lead. Your own friends . . . boyfriends.'

She gave a fluttery little laugh that echoed around the patio and grated on Anya's already raw nerves. She couldn't speak. There was a lump in her throat. Just then Rose came out of the house to take the children in for their tea, and Althea rose elegantly and began to come across to them.

Helen would care for them, if that was the right word to use. They would have all that was necessary for life and comfort, everything money could buy, but what of their emotional comfort? There would be no real love, just a gradual possession. And yet Anya couldn't say that. She couldn't say anything at all. They were Zack's children, and Helen was Zack's mother.

Althea smiled down at her. 'Do you feel better after your walk, Anya?'

She nodded and then got to her feet. 'I'm going to my room,' she said in a choked voice. 'I don't want any dinner.'

'About the children . . . you do see it's for the best, don't you? You don't want to waste your youth with such responsibilities.'

'It must be as Zack wants it,' she murmured as she turned to go.

Unconcernedly Althea unfurled herself into the beach chair. Anya wondered how anyone could remain so cool and calm. Inwardly she was screaming. Screaming because Cèlie had died, screaming because they were all determined to think Jared guilty of her murder, and worst of all, because Althea and Helen were, between them, successfully separating her from Zack.

10

When Anya finally came downstairs that evening, having grown bored with her own company and the incessant thoughts that passed through her mind, it was to hear Zack's voice raised in anger. She came down the stairs slowly, anxious not to intrude on a private argument, although the hall of the villa was hardly the place to conduct any kind of private business.

Zack had showered and shaved since she had last seen him and he was once again dressed in his customary style of elegance. The white and haggard look had gone from his face which was now suffused with colour.

Anya was no longer afraid of walking in on an angry scene; she was openly curious to see who was outside, behind the half-closed front door. If Zack had possessed the required strength he would have closed it completely, shutting out whoever was trying to gain admittance.

When she reached the bottom step she was shocked and surprised to hear a familiar voice say, 'At least have the grace to tell her I'm here.'

'There's no point, Nolan. She's not going out with you again. You may as well know now, as soon as the inquest is over my family is going back to England.'

'Zack — Jared,' said Anya, hurrying forward, 'what is going on here?'

Zack turned round abruptly and the door was pushed open so she could see Jared at last.

'I was just telling this fellow that you're not seeing him again.'

Anya stiffened. 'I shall decide who I see and who I don't see, Zack. Come inside, Jared.'

He stepped into the hall looking ruffled for once and he shot an angry look at the other man.

'Now,' said Anya, 'perhaps one of you

189

will tell me what is going on.'

'I only want to take you out this evening,' Jared told her. 'I thought you would like to get out for a while.'

'I would be failing in my duty if I allowed you to,' Zack said.

Anya threw back her head in a gesture of defiance. 'Don't sound so pompous, Zack. You are not responsible for me. I am responsible for myself. And I wish you would stop this ridiculous nonsense about Jared.'

Zack's eyes burned darkly in their sockets. 'Your safety is more than a responsibility, Anya.'

Jared reached out for her hand and she flashed him a grateful smile. 'Come along, Anya. A few hours of relaxation will do you good.'

'I'd love to, Jared,' she answered eagerly, 'only I have to look after the children.'

He didn't let go of her hand, but he did look at the other man. 'I'm sure there are a number of responsible adults who are capable of looking in on two sleeping children for the next two or three hours.'

'But I'm not dressed for dining out.'

'We're not going to the Ritz.'

He drew her through the open doorway and she had to run to keep up with him until they reached the car. Neither of them paused even when the door slammed shut behind them.

As he handed her into the car he said, smiling, 'You're improving. A few days ago you would have obeyed him.'

'You're wrong,' she retorted. 'I've always been my own mistress.'

'That's only because you haven't met your master yet.'

★   ★   ★

The downstairs lights were off when they returned, but most of the bedroom lights were still alight. Despite her protest that she wasn't hungry Jared had taken her to a small bistro in St. Raphael where he had ordered bouillabaisse which much to her surprise, she had enjoyed. A trio played raucous music and many of the diners danced, or sang, or clapped along with them, which precluded almost all conversation and yet diverted her mind.

It seemed that Jared knew just the place to take her on this occasion. It pleased her that he was sensitive to her moods and it had only just occurred to her that he did understand her well, very well indeed. The sureness of his every word and act was a foil to her own habitual uncertainty.

When they returned to the villa Anya remained in the car. There was no urgency for her to go inside. The memory of the cloud they were all under seemed more oppressive when she was inside the villa.

They hadn't exchanged a word since leaving St. Raphael but now Anya looked at him at last. 'Did Inspector Sandray come to see you this afternoon, Jared?'

He turned a fraction and there was a small smile playing around the corners of his lips. 'Now you're spoiling yourself.'

'I'm sorry. I can't help it. It's haunting me — the whole business. I've never known anyone who's been murdered before.'

His smile didn't falter and yet she had the feeling he was deadly serious. 'Or anyone under suspicion?'

'Did he come?'

'Of course. He asked me a few questions and then went away again. He's a very civil man. I think he'll catch whoever it was.'

Anya shivered. 'I wish the inquest was over so we could go home. Zack's closing the villa up this year. We're not staying for the rest of the summer.'

'Are you glad about that?'

'At the moment I can't wait to be away from here, but Helen intends to take charge of the children herself — with an army of helpers, no doubt. I'm not very happy about that.'

His interest quickened then. *'I'm*

delighted to hear it. It's the best thing for you.'

'But not for the children.'

'You can't live everyone else's life for them.'

'I can have a darned good try. I'd better go inside. The atmosphere is horrible now. It wasn't so good before — not with Marika gone — but at least I got on with Zack . . . '

'The handsome prince has turned back into a frog, hmm?'

Anya let out a gasp of annoyance. 'That isn't the right analogy, Jared. We're all out of sorts at the moment.'

'It's me,' he said bluntly. 'You disagree over me.'

Anya played with the strap of her handbag. 'He means it for the best. He thinks he's protecting me. Looking at it from his point of view, he's right.'

She started to get out of the car but Jared put his hand over her arm to stop her. 'Don't go yet.' She hesitated and looked at him. 'I'd rather you didn't go back there at all, Anya.'

She sank back into her seat. 'What? What do you mean? I've already told you I won't stay on your boat.'

He shook his head. 'Not on the boat, Anya. In an hotel. I'll drive you to Toulon and book you into an hotel. You can leave a message at the villa and let the police know where you are if they need to question you.'

Anya stared at him, wondering if he had taken leave of his senses. 'Why on earth would I do a thing like that?'

He stared at her, gravely and his grey eyes looked very dark. He was suddenly very much older, not so much the charming companion, the amusing diversion, but a man in his own right. An attractive man too. She had noticed that before but only in a detached way. Now her heart was beating unevenly beneath her ribs, just as it had done this afternoon on the boat, and she wasn't detached at all. And the feeling was no less intense because the night with its own particularly intimate sounds was all

195

around, and they were in their own little capsule of light.

'Jared?' she whispered uncertainly.

He came closer, slipping his arm around her with a slow deliberation. She moved closer to him, to meet him halfway and her eyes closed long before his lips met hers. He took a long time to kiss her but once begun Anya wanted it to go on for ever. With him there was no panic, just the utter bliss of someone who had waited a long time for this to happen.

'Damn these silly little French cars!' he said at last. 'What I wouldn't give to have my own car here right now.'

They were still very close, only a hair's breadth away from each other. She giggled. 'I bet you have a very special model, equipped with every aid to seduction.'

'You're suggesting I do this all the time.'

He began to kiss her again, and Anya wondered why she had wasted the past few days in his company, for their chaste little relationship seemed a sad waste now.

'It does happen quickly, just as you said it can,' she whispered.

'That's what I was trying to tell you. I'm glad you've realised it at last. I was beginning to despair.'

He drew away again, smoothed her hair from her face and said softly, 'You do see now why I want you away from the villa. I don't want to lose you now.'

She warmed to the tenderness in his eyes, touched his lips with the tips of her fingers and said, 'You're not going to lose me, not until you're heartily sick and tired of me.'

'That will be never.'

'Seriously though . . . '

'I've never been more serious.'

'It's all over with Zack. You knew that it would be, didn't you?'

'That isn't what's bothering me.' He drew away even further and she felt bereft, wanting him near to her while this feeling of wonderment was still so new to her; so new and wonderful the

197

dark veil of the past half day seemed partially lifted although she felt, whatever was in store for her in the future, the horror of Cèlie's fate would remain with her all her life.

'Heaven knows, the last thing I want to do now is upset you, but — I don't know how to say this. I'll have to be brutal.'

Suddenly panic was rising inside her. She sat up sharply clenching her fists together. 'They're not going to arrest you!'

He smiled faintly in the darkness. 'Not as far as I know. They don't usually give notice of it if they are.'

He reached out and took her hand in his. Immediately she felt warmer. 'What did you mean by being brutal then?'

'In the past year three people have died — Paulette Duvaloir, your sister and Cèlie. The villa and its inhabitants seems to be the common denominator in all three deaths.'

'Paulette Duvaloir has nothing to do with the villa,' she said, licking her lips which had suddenly become dry.

'She died not far away.'

'She was murdered. Marika was accidently drowned. There was no question of anything else!'

He held her hand more tightly as she attempted in her panic to draw it from him. 'Listen to me, Anya. It seems odd that your sister should disregard a storm warning and go swimming despite it.'

'She was upset that morning. Everyone saw that she was upset although she refused to say why.'

'Well, even disregarding your sister, there have been two murders in this vicinity, and two murderers would be too much of a coincidence. I want you away from here where I can keep an eye on you. I don't know anything about the motive for these crimes. There may be more to them than we know about.' He looked uncompromisingly grim, something so unusual for him that it made her more afraid than ever. 'But on the other hand it may be the work of a common or garden sex maniac who couldn't get what he wanted; in which case I'd rather know where you are. When someone kills, each time it gets easier for them.'

Anya sat up straight again, her eyes filling with horror. 'You can't mean to infer that someone at the villa may be responsible.'

He didn't answer; he just kept on staring ahead into the darkness. Anya's mind whirled in endless circles.

'There's only Gervase and he's the gentlest of men, Jared. Besides, he's very happily married, and has a grown-up family; grandchildren too, I believe. You must be wrong.'

He looked at her then. 'I wasn't particularly thinking of Gervase.'

She shrank away from him. 'Oh no, Jared, you're wrong.'

'Most people are like you, Anya. They don't want to believe people they know are capable of anything bad, which makes me wonder why your friends at the villa were so quick to label me a murderer. It may be, perhaps, they know each other to be capable of such an act and the only way they can blot out the fear is to point the finger at someone outside. None of them have very good alibis.'

'Zack was in his study all afternoon.'

'So he says.'

'He's incapable of hurting anyone. He was so ill when he had to go and identify her.'

'And the women?'

Anya was about to defend them too but she hesitated. 'I have the feeling that Althea and Helen could both be ruthless if necessary to get what they wanted, but *this* . . . there's no reason. Oh, Jared, you're wrong!'

She looked at him appealingly but all he said was, 'I hope so. It's very likely that I am, but I'd still like you to come with me — *now*, Anya.'

She drew to the far side of the car and then let him take her into his arms again, returning his kisses with a new ardour, an almost desperate passion.

When she drew away again she said,
'Don't ask me to, Jared. I'm needed
here. When this is over — when the
inquest's over — I'll come with you
anywhere you wish.' Her eyes filled with
tears. 'I'm frightened, Jared. Not
because of what you've said; I don't
believe it is anyone we know. I firmly
believe that. But I am frightened for
you. I can see it the way the French
police will see it. I'm afraid they'll take
you away from me.'

He gripped both her unsteady hands
in his. 'No one is going to do that. I
have to make an official statement to
the police tomorrow but as soon as I'm
finished there I'll come to you. I'll stay
with you all day.' His voice softened.
'We'll go down to the beach, just the
two of us.'

She nodded happily. 'That will be
marvellous. Poor Cèlie, if it hadn't been
for what has happened to her we might
never . . . '

He kissed her lips lightly to stop her
speaking. 'Yes, we would.

'Promise me, Anya, when I'm not with you you'll stay in company. Don't wander off on your own.'

'I'll just sit by the pool with the children and think about you.'

'I approve of that,' he said, kissing her briefly. Then he looked at her. 'This is one hell of a time to start something as good as this.' He drew her close again and she clung on to him tightly, almost with desperation. His lips were in her hair as he murmured, 'Much as I'd like to keep you here, if you're determined you'd better go now.'

He walked with her to the door of the villa. 'Are you sure you won't change your mind?'

She shook her head and slid her arms around his neck. 'I couldn't. Please understand. I know them far better than you, and I know there's no need for me to be afraid.'

He gave her one last kiss and insisted that she go inside while he waited, but she stayed in the hall until she heard his car start up some distance from the building. Then she sighed. She wasn't sure why; whether it was through happiness or fear.

She went slowly up the stairs, trying to pinpoint the start of this marvellous thing that had happened between them. It was impossible to recall the start of the miracle of love. It had happened and that was sufficient. Life would be intolerable now without him and yet only a short time ago she was so sure her happiness depended on Zack.

The upper hall was thickly carpeted and so her sandalled feet made no sound as she walked. It was late, she knew, and yet she had never felt less like sleeping. This totally new awareness his kisses had awakened in her drove weariness away. She wanted to remain alert, to recall every inflexion of his voice, every expression that crossed his face. She felt as if she were standing at the edge of a chasm of infinite joy and together with Jared she would drown in it.

The carpet muffled her footsteps

effectively and yet, instinctively, Anya walked carefully. Part of her wanted to tell everyone immediately about her new relationship with Jared, but part of her also cried out for caution; that it was best for it to remain her secret for a little while longer.

She was already past Zack's room when she heard laughter — female laughter. She hesitated, puzzled for the moment, and then the laughter came again. Anya's face flooded with colour. She recognised Althea's voice. Anya felt she shouldn't be surprised; Althea had already as much as admitted she would do anything to win Zack's affection.

Anya was about to move on when the door opened. Althea was still smiling as she closed it carefully behind her. She looked up and when she saw Anya her smile faltered momentarily.

'Hello, Anya. Had a nice evening?'

Anya straightened up. 'Fine, thank you. I see you've been enjoying yourself too.'

Althea chuckled softly. Her immaculate tresses were now tumbled in disarray around her shoulders. She wore a pale pink dressing-gown, functional and a little austere, and yet in it Althea managed to look handsome. Such looks as she possessed would last longer than conventional prettiness. Althea would always be handsome.

'I told you you couldn't win,' she said as she tightened her dressing-gown around her in a strangely sensual gesture. 'People are terribly conventional, even these days, so we've been circumspect, but it has been going on rather a long time.'

She hesitated, eyeing Anya's frozen features curiously. 'I hope you won't take this too much to heart.'

'Don't worry, I won't,' Anya answered in a harsh whisper. She felt sickened, not at Althea's affair but because Zack had made vague promises which he had no intention of fulfilling.

'I'm glad, really glad. I told you I was more suited to Zack than you . . .'

'I believe you.'

Althea gave a little disparaging laugh. 'I don't just love him blindly, Anya. His talent — his fame — means little to you, but it means more than anything else to Zack, and it means a great deal to me.'

Anya turned away. She was tired now. 'Justify it as you wish.'

The other girl moved across the corridor to her own room and just as she put her hand on the door knob Anya stopped and said in a voice only just above a whisper, 'You said it's been going on a long time . . . was it when Marika was alive?'

She smiled and her features softened. 'Don't fret. It started at Christmas in London.' Anya sighed with relief and as Althea opened the door she added wryly, 'I had no intention of being the 'other woman', Anya. before Marika died there was nothing in it for me.'

For a moment Anya was frozen into immobility as she recalled Jared's fears for her, and Althea's determination to marry Zack. Her mind just wouldn't frame the thought. She was blindly aware that the other girl was smiling still.

'You know, Anya, despite your professed fondness for Zack, your lipstick is smeared.'

She went into her room and closed the door. Anya's fingers flew to her lips and then she realised, she hadn't been wearing any lipstick this evening.

11

The birds were singing merrily in the orange tree outside the nursery window when Anya awoke the next morning. Since Cèlie's disappearance she had slept in her room although when she had learned of the girl's death she shrank from sleeping in the same bed. But once the police had finished searching it Sylvie and Gervase had packed all of her things and had taken them down to the basement. Now there was no trace left of Cèlie's existence in the villa and it depressed Anya to see how quickly one's identity can be obliterated simply by removing a few worldly possessions.

Anya came round slowly from sleep after having found difficulty in falling asleep in the first place. She stretched lazily, her senses telling her it was much later than her usual time for waking, but then, she reminded herself, times were unusual. She was in love, hopelessly and finally in love, and no tragedy could overshadow the innate joy she felt when she thought of Jared and the promise in his kiss.

A slight sound reached her from the children's room and she sat up sharply, coming out of her reverie at last. She swung her legs over the side of the bed, drew on her dressing-gown and padded quickly to where she thought the children were still sleeping, but when she pushed open the door Anya received a shock; Althea was watching Rose put Jason and Penny into their best clothes. She was dressed in a smartly styled dress and jacket of sapphire blue which suited her glacial looks so well.

She looked rather pleased with herself. In fact the little smile that played at the edges of her mouth reminded Anya quite painfully of Cèlie's self-satisfied smile, and she was repulsed.

'Oh, I hope we didn't disturb you,' she said when she saw Anya. 'We thought we'd let you sleep on this morning.'

'We're going to Toulon!' Jason piped up excitedly.

'Toulon,' echoed his sister, 'with best shoes.'

'And we're going to have *lunch* out with Granny!'

Anya smiled at him. 'How marvellous, darling. You'll be able to have an enormous ice-cream if you eat all your lunch.'

'Can we go out one day with you and Uncle Jared?' he asked.

'Where's Uncle Jared?' said Penny, looking bewildered.

'Go along and find Granny,' said Althea pleasantly. 'You too, Rose; take them downstairs and I'll join you all in a few moments.'

Anya kissed the children goodbye and felt her heart warm at the way they clung to her despite their excitement at the coming treat.

When they had gone Anya looked

sharply at Althea. 'What's going on now, Althea?'

Althea laughed softly. 'Nothing is *going on*. Mrs. Anderson decided that the children needed some articles of clothing; new shoes and so forth. So we're taking them to Toulon and making it into a treat for them. And Zack doesn't feel like working today, so . . . I'm going along too. We're taking Rose too, to make sure they behave themselves.' She went to the door. 'Do you need anything I can get you while I'm out?'

Anya looked away, her thoughts in a whirl. Until it was thought she would be caring for the children no one was interested in them. Now it seemed both Althea and Helen realised their importance to Zack.

If it weren't for the children themselves she wouldn't care, but they were too precious to be used as pawns.

'There's nothing, Althea. I may go shopping myself later in the week.'

When she had gone Anya felt

dispirited again. There was nothing she could possibly do; that was the awful part of it. Neither Althea nor Helen had any real affection for Jason and Penny, just a desire to have a firmer hold on Zack's affections.

As she showered and dressed, Anya cheered herself by thinking of Jared, wondering when he would come. As soon as he could, she didn't doubt, but he was with the police and there was no way of knowing how long he would be there, unless . . . She shuddered. No. There was nothing to fear for Jared. He was innocent and no one could prove otherwise.

When she went downstairs the villa was unusually quiet. She remembered Jared urging her to stay in company, but she shrugged off his misgivings. Cèlie's death had unbalanced all their thoughts.

She was about to go to the kitchen to get some coffee and a roll, which was as much as she could manage this morning, when she saw Zack coming up the basement stairs. There was a worried frown marring his usually bland features, but when he saw Anya it gave way to a smile.

'Hello, stranger,' he said softly.

She smiled uncertainly. 'Hello, Zack.'

It was some relief to find him in an affable mood and she was glad she had waited for him to speak first. In the back of her mind she had been worrying how to approach him after the events of last night.

'I'm sorry about last night, Anya,' he said a moment later. 'I was only trying to protect you.'

She relaxed. 'I understand, Zack. I realise that you meant it for the best, and feelings were running a little high all round.'

'It's a sorry business, but I don't suppose we can allow it to blight all our lives. I've always believed victims are never entirely innocent. There's always something to invite their fate.'

'How cynical you are, Zack. She was only eighteen.'

'Old enough to sin in many ways.' She glanced at the half open door to the basement and he smiled grimly, 'I was just getting Cèlie's things ready to be sent back to her parents.'

'Can't Gervase do that?'

'I suppose so,' he admitted, 'but it gave me something to do. I can't write at the moment with people coming and going all the time, wanting to speak to me. There have been some newspaper men around this morning, but I managed to get rid of them for the moment. I need peace and tranquillity,' he went on, sighing deeply. 'Do you think it will ever return? Sometimes I think there's a curse on this damned place. I'm thinking very seriously of selling it.'

'I couldn't understand why you didn't last year, after Marika . . . '

'I wish I had,' he sighed, yet again. He looked old just then, much older than his thirty-seven years. 'It may not be so easy now. Not after *two* deaths have been associated with it. People are superstitious about things like that.'

'Well, at least you should have peace today,' she told him in a gentle voice. In many ways Zack was like a child. 'We have the house to ourselves, I believe.'

His face brightened then. 'It's absolutely wonderful the way Mother and Althea have taken an interest in the children lately.'

'Only since it was feared *I* was going to look after them, that I would have their undivided affection.'

He smiled foolishly. He *was* like a child. 'Oh no, Anya. It's not that at all. Mother was quite concerned about you having to give up opportunities, the enjoyment of youth.'

'Don't be foolish, Zack,' she snapped and his smile disappeared. 'Can't you see they're using Jason and Penny as a claim on you? Helen would do anything rather than let you marry again but she and Althea have come to some kind of unspoken agreement.' She smiled grimly. 'They're going to share you, and because they're so determined I don't believe there's a thing you or I can do about it. As Julius Caesar said, 'The die is cast'.'

'It's you I'm interested in, Anya,' he said. 'You know that already.'

He put his hand on her arm and she looked down at it with distaste, but she made no attempt to remove it. 'I know you've been having an affaire with Althea since Christmas.'

He let her arm go and his face contorted with such unexpected fury that Anya quailed. 'She told you!'

'She didn't have to, Zack. I saw her coming out of your room last night when I came back from St. Raphael.'

His anger went as quickly as it had come. 'I'll finish it, Anya. Today. As soon as she comes back. I promise you that.'

'Don't finish it on my account.' She was unable to look at him. 'My affections, as they say, are engaged elsewhere.'

His eyes narrowed. 'Nolan?' She nodded and he gripped her arms

217

tightly, turning her round so that she had to face him. 'How serious is it?'

'Very.' She raised her eyes to his. 'I'm in love with him.'

'And what are his feelings in the matter?' His lips twisted into a sneer of sheer disbelief. 'Does he feel the same way about you?'

'Yes.' It came out as a long sigh.

He let her go. 'Does he want to marry you?'

'I don't know yet. It's too soon. But if he asks me, I will. Gladly. The children no longer need me, do they?'

'Neither does he,' Zack said, looking down at the floor. 'But I do, and believe it or not, the children do too.'

She was already moving away from him. 'No, you don't, Zack. You're just like a child who doesn't want to share his toys. And as for the children, I don't want to be around to watch them being used.'

'Anya!' She stopped. 'I didn't want to tell you this, but Inspector Sandray told me in confidence that he suspected

Nolan very strongly of having killed Cèlie. He hasn't told the truth in some matters and the police are having a thorough investigation made in Canada.'

She felt a lump form in her throat. She thought of Jared, his grey eyes, so frank and open. He was incapable of deceit, let alone anything more serious.

'They won't find anything wrong in Jared's background,' she said, willing back the tears that were springing to her eyes.

'I'm trying to save you being hurt, Anya,' he pleaded. 'That man is going to hurt you badly.'

'No,' she gasped, and as he came towards her she began to run. She would never believe Jared guilty of any wrongdoing. Never.

★　★　★

Breakfast turned out to be half a cup of coffee, for that was all she could possibly manage. Afterwards, leaving Sylvie to her baking, Anya walked disconsolately on to the patio. She saw Zack stretched out on an air bed, reading a newspaper. He was completely engrossed in it. She turned away; she had enjoyed enough of his company this morning.

Most of her clothing and personal belongings were still in the room she had occupied up until Cèlie's disappearance, and she decided that now was as good a time as any to transfer the more necessary items of her wardrobe to the nursery. Wryly Anya realised that she wouldn't need to occupy it for long; Helen would soon whisk the children away, out of her life completely. And if Jared meant to marry her and take her back to Canada with him, then, Anya knew, she would have no jurisidiction over them at all.

It was a terrible dilemma for Anya who knew, even if she were not to go with Jared, she could do little for them apart from occasional visits, and she just could not bear to give up her new love; she would stay with him for as long as he wanted her.

Children were resilient, she told herself. They had borne their mother's death remarkably well. Perhaps the outlook wasn't so bleak; perhaps they would grow up with more spirit than their father.

As she transferred her clothes from one wardobe to the other, she could hear one of the maids singing as she vacuumed Althea's room. A small pile of clean linen had been left on Anya's bed and she quickly transferred it to one of the drawers in the dresser. She closed the drawer firmly, only to find that it would not shut completely. Anya pulled it open again, impatiently, and then heard something drop down at the back of it. Puzzled, as the drawer contained only items of underwear, she pulled it out completely and after setting it down on the bed felt around at the back of the dresser.

Anya stared in amazement at the gold locket she had withdrawn. The case was chased gold and it dangled on a fine chain which had been broken at the clasp. She wondered how long it had been trapped at the back of that drawer as she turned it over and over in her hand. After a moment or two she prised it open. Two photographs lay in the palm of her hand. Two familiar faces stared up at her, jumping unnaturally in front of her eyes.

Slowly, shocked numb, she sank down on to the bed, trying to work out what this meant, but her mind was not functioning very well. One of the photographs was very familiar to her. She had seen that same laughing face in Cèlie's magazine — Paulette Duvaloir. The other photograph Anya couldn't bear to look at again. She closed her eyes but she could still see his face clearly in front of her. His hair was shorter, his face thinner. He was a few years younger on the photograph, but with that smile it was unmistakably Jared.

She buried her face in her hands, shaking with silent sobs. Zack for all his faults had been right. She had fallen in love with a man who had abundant charm and was a plausible liar — and perhaps he was even worse than that. Without doubt, now, Anya knew he *was* worse than that.

The locket lay closed now on the bed at her side. Suddenly she jumped up and with shaking hands groped at the back of the dresser until her trembling fingers located something she had vaguely noticed before — a crumpled envelope. It was addressed to someone she had never heard of — someone who lived in Lyon. Hastily Anya unfolded the letter inside and to her frustration found the words written on the single sheet were French. She sank down on to the bed again and forced herself to concentrate on what was written.

So brief a happiness, she thought bitterly as the tears she fought to contain blurred the pages of the letter. Oh, Jared, she cried inwardly, did you talk of love so convincingly to Paulette Duvaloir and Cèlie?

'My dearest friend,' she translated, 'I am writing this hurriedly and trust you to understand that I am entrusting you with this locket and so, you will realise, entrusting you with my life. He says now that he only wants the locket, but I see that if I give it to him my life will no longer be safe. So keep it safe for me. He will pay me again so that I don't give him away. I may just have found treasure trove! Cèlie.'

Anya crumpled the paper in her hands and let it fall to the floor. Then she clenched the locket in her fist and ran out of the room and down the stairs, brushing away her tears with her free hand.

Zack looked up with a start when she came running out of the salon on to the patio. The sun was shining out of a cloudless sky today — a typical Riviera day. The brightness of its rays beating down on the tiled surround to the pool and on the rippleless water mocked her. Everything that lived mocked her; the jasmine in the garden edging the pool, the multi-hued roses, and the red of the bougainvillaea which spilled like blood over the white walls of the villa. Anya would never before have believed misery could be so profound.

'Sweetie, what is it?'

Anya felt as though her legs would carry her no farther and she sank down into a chair facing him. She held out the locket in both hands as he frowned at her worriedly.

'You were right, Zack! It was Jared. He must have killed Paulette Duvaloir too. He was being blackmailed by Cèlie. That's why he killed her. Oh, Zack, what am I to do now?'

He took the locket from her and turned it over slowly in his hands as if mesmerised by it. 'Where on earth did you find this?'

'At the back of one of the drawers in the dresser in the nursery. Cèlie must have pushed it back there for safety. It fell down when I closed the drawer after I'd been putting my own things in.'

'The police can't have made a very

thorough search of that room if they didn't find this. Still, we are in France, and they're not exactly efficient.'

'Zack, tell me what to do, please!' she begged. 'I must take it to the police. Oh, heavens, how ironic that it should be me who found it!'

Zack suddenly snapped out of his reverie. 'I tried to warn you, Sweetie. I shudder to think of the chances you've taken. He must be desperate and quite dangerous by now.'

'I believed everything he said,' she murmured bitterly, staring unseeingly into space. Then she looked at Zack who was watching her anxiously, 'Will you come with me to see Inspector Sandray? I don't think I could face him on my own.'

Zack pocketed the locket. 'You realise what it will mean, don't you?'

Anya covered her face in a useless attempt to blot out the thought. 'Yes!'

'Look, Anya,' he said thoughtfully, 'it will mean a lot more unpleasantness for us all. We'll be involved even further and we'll be stuck here in France for months. It's probable that the police will arrest him anyway, so perhaps we don't have to turn this over at all. Perhaps we don't have to be involved any further in this matter.'

Anya's hands dropped into her lap as she stared at him in astonishment. 'Whatever he is, Anya, knowing you as I do, I realise your feelings for him are deep and genuine. You don't want to be the instrument of his arrest, do you?'

'You know I don't, Zack, but I must do my duty. Don't you see, someone else might be at risk. I'd never forgive myself if . . . '

He stood up and put his hand beneath her elbow. 'Let's walk a bit and talk this over rationally. If we stay here we might be interrupted.'

She had no will of her own. She let him lead her away from the pool. They walked as far as the cliff edge where he sat down on the wall and she did likewise. A row of cypress trees screened them from view, tall and majestic, and suddenly sinister when she recalled that these trees were often used in graveyards.

'Sweetie, murder in France is still punishable by death, at the very least by life imprisonment.'

'I don't want to hear!'

She put her hands over her ears but she could still hear him when he said a moment later, 'After all it's only a locket with photographs of Nolan and the Duvaloir girl. It doesn't mean all that much on its own.'

'It shows they were connected. That must be her locket . . . ' She stopped and looked up slowly. 'Zack, you didn't look inside the locket. How did you know what was . . . ?'

His expression did not change. He reached out and, putting his arm around her shoulders, drew her closer. Anya had no will to draw away.

'You told me what was inside.'

Anya felt panic rise inside her, recalling Zack's unease the morning of Cèlie's death; Zack coming up from the basement where Cèlie's belongings were put.

'I didn't, Zack!' she cried. 'I didn't say what was inside and you didn't open it just now, but you knew!'

He drew a sigh of resignation. 'I've been so careful, Anya, so lucky and so careful. I knew it couldn't go on for ever. It's a nightmare that's with me all the time.'

She looked into the face that was so familiar to her. The burning dark eyes of artistic talent, the skin that was really too smooth for a man, the wide, sensitive mouth. He looked exactly the same as usual, and that in itself was terrifying to Anya.

'Zack, you didn't . . . ' Her eyes opened wide in horror as the full realism came to her belatedly. 'Why, Zack? Why?'

He looked down behind him, down to the beach where Anya had first met Jared Nolan. Jared who was in some way connected with Paulette Duvaloir and yet who was innocent of her murder. Amidst the horror of this new discovery that fact was singing loudly and joyously in her ears.

'I met Paulette Duvaloir last summer. She wasn't the first little *amor* I'd had since I married Marika, but none of them were serious. Paulette was different. She had integrity, I suppose. She didn't know I was married, and she believed everything I told her. I don't think she ever realised that I was meeting her furtively.

'Then she found out I was married — someone in St. Brilac had been talking about us. She was furious — mostly because I'd deceived her. She threatened to make a scene in public to teach me a lesson.'

He looked at Anya now. She was too numb to feel revulsion. She could only wonder why she hadn't seen this side of him before. Did Althea know? Or Helen?

'I'm a celebrity of sorts, Anya. I've seen the way the French press treat us. It would make a horrible mess. Before I knew what was happening she was lying on the ground and I had her locket in my hand. I was in a state of shock, Anya; I was horrified at what I'd done. I should have dropped the locket on the ground but I pushed it instead into my pocket and forgot about it.

'There was publicity and a police investigation. No one suspected me. Why should they? After a while I allowed myself to relax. I was safe. And then about three weeks later Marika must have been preparing some clothes for the cleaner; she probably found it in my pocket then.'

His face contorted. 'She knew what it meant, of course. The police had been looking for that locket ever since they found Paulette. Marika must have deliberately gone out for a swim in the storm; anything, probably, rather than face up to what I'd done. I realised all this, of course, when I went to find the locket and saw that it was gone. I knew then that Marika had found it.'

'Oh, Zack. Oh, heavens, Marika,' was all Anya could say. She was physically sick and she was fighting back the nausea.

'I turned the villa upside down trying to find that locket, I convinced myself after a while that Marika had taken it into the sea with her, until Cèlie found it amongst some of Penny's toys. In her shock Marika must have just left it lying around and Penny, or Jason, probably picked it up. It had been in the nursery all that time.

'Oh, Cèlie was a bright one. She recognised Paulette and realised she had a piece of evidence the police had been searching for for a year. She knew how to make capital out of that.'

'You paid her.'

'Yes, I paid her, and well. She knew just how to cash in on those fears that had haunted me all that time. And then Nolan arrived. I suspected that he was connected with the case the moment you told me he was from Canada, and then when I found out he was from

Quebec, I *knew*. She was from Quebec — Paulette.

'I went down to St. Brilac when everyone thought I was working and waited until he came off the boat. I recognised him from the photograph in the locket. I began to wonder, then, if she hadn't written to him at the time to tell him about us and he had bided his time until he could come and accuse me himself. I didn't know what to think!'

'You tried to kill him that day. You would have pushed him overboard if I hadn't come along early and surprised you.'

'He was heavier than I imagined. It was a panic measure. I told you I didn't know what to think. I didn't dare try again, though. I'm not brave, Anya. I've been so scared. There's no end to it, you know.'

'I can't believe it's true,' she moaned. 'Not you, Zack. Not you.'

'When I look back it's almost as if it *is* some other person. Not me at all. I've never wanted to hurt anyone in my life before. And when I think of Marika . . . '

'Poor Cèlie too.'

His voice hardened. 'You don't have to feel sorry for her. As long as I kept on paying her I knew she was reasonably trustworthy. But then Nolan came and she recognised him from the photograph, just as I did. I knew she was trying to work out how she could benefit by him too, so I agreed on a final price, for the locket itself. We made arrangements to meet and I would pay over the money and she would give me the locket. But she took the money but said the locket was her insurance. She didn't dare hand it over to me. I had to kill her. I knew I had no alternative.

'After it was over I took the money back and searched her bag, but, of course, it wasn't there. I was mad to believe it would be. I came back and searched her room, too, just as the police did. I was frantic by then.'

He sighed. 'You don't realise what a relief it is just to be able to talk about it, Anya. I could always talk to you, though.'

'You'd have let Jared take the blame, wouldn't you?' she said, her voice suddenly stronger, suddenly harsh.

'I'd be mad not to.'

'You're mad all right,' she said, her face contorting with bitterness. 'But no one else is going to be . . . hurt by finding that locket. You've finished . . . destroying, Zack.'

He stared at her. 'Anya, you're not going to tell anyone about it.'

'No,' she said reasonably, looking away for fear that her eyes would betray her. It had only just come to her that she was in danger too now. From Zack! It was horrible. 'No, I won't tell anyone. I promise.'

'I don't think I really believe you,' he said softly in her ear.

She felt his arm tighten around her shoulders as she tried to move away from him. She opened her mouth to speak but he clapped one firm hand over it and began to pull her backwards — over the wall, down on to those cruel crags. Just now, as the sun passed behind a cloud, it looked as if the red of them was staining the sea with blood. Soon there would be her blood.

He had her in a vice-like grip so that she couldn't even struggle, and she certainly couldn't scream for help. The fear of what was going to happen to her went straight to her head and Anya knew she was going to faint. If she did, she knew she would be lost. Instinctively she wanted to put her head between her knees or she was going to lose consciousness fast, but it was no use trying; Zack was pulling her backwards. The wall was no longer beneath her and she was falling, falling, falling, down into the infinite blackness of the sea.

★ ★ ★

'Anya, Anya, my love, can you hear me?'

The pleading voice seemed to come from a long way away, and she wanted to reach out for it, to cling on to it, for it meant safety. She tried to open her eyes but it was her lips that parted and she began to cough and splutter as a vile-tasting liquid trickled down her throat.

'At last,' came a heartfelt cry. 'Anya, can you hear me?'

'Of course I can,' she murmured as she opened her eyes at last. Jared smiled at her uncertainly with concern in his eyes. She was lying, incredibly, on the sofa inside the villa.

He put the glass of brandy down and turned back to her, taking her hands in his. 'I thought you were never going to come round.'

'Zack, he . . . '

'I know. Don't think about it.'

'I went over the edge.'

'No, I thought you were going to but he let you go when he saw us and you pitched forward instead. I don't ever want to have a fright like that again. I

237

thought I was never going to reach you. Like one of those dreams when you're trying to run and you can't.'

She sat up, choking back a sob. 'What's happened to Zack? He was going to . . .'

'But he didn't. He saw us coming and he instinctively moved backwards and tripped over the wall. There was nothing anyone could do to stop him. I'm so sorry, Anya.'

For the second time he held her while she cried on his shoulder.

'I always seem to be doing this,' she sobbed as he handed her his handkerchief.

'This is the last time,' he promised. 'From now on it's all smiles for us.'

'I don't think that's possible now. Too much has happened. He killed twice! Zack, of all people. He would have killed you and me.'

'I know most of the story now, Anya. Don't distress yourself by talking about it.'

'What will Helen do now? Poor

Helen. He's ruined so many people who loved him.'

'Helen knows. She came back just afterwards.' Anya drew back and looked at him. He smiled faintly. 'Shopping with two little kids didn't turn out the joy-ride she'd anticipated. They felt sick in the car and Penny wanted the toilet several times. She and Althea decided they weren't going to enjoy it very much after all so they turned back.'

'Does she know about Zack? All about it, I mean.'

He sighed. 'Yes, she knows. If you ask me I think she had her suspicions all the time.'

Anya asked in a whisper, 'How did she take it, Jared?'

He sighed. 'I'm afraid not very well. A doctor had to be called to give her a sedative. It was fortunate the police had sent for one anyway, to attend to . . . Anderson. He looked at you too and said you'd only fainted, which was a great relief, but you were out too long for my liking.'

'And Althea?'

'She is the most remarkable woman. She's coping now with the children in the most admirable way — with the help of Rose and Sylvie, of course. I think she's glad of something to do. They all are.'

Anya felt the tears welling up in her eyes again. 'How did you manage to arrive on time? A minute or two later . . . '

He looked grim. 'I'd rather you did not remind me of that, Anya. I came with Inspector Sandray. He was coming to arrest your brother-in-law.' Anya's eyes grew wider and Jared smiled sadly. 'Yes, I know you thought I was the obvious suspect, but there was quite a lot of evidence against Anderson this time. He'd made quite a lot of withdrawals from his bank account whereas Cèlie had made deposits of almost identical amounts. There was other evidence too; soil on the tyres of his car — that sort of thing — and a letter Cèlie's friend in Lyon received

240

three or four weeks ago telling her all about it. He wasn't very clever. It was just sheer luck that he got away with Paulette's murder.'

'When I found the locket I thought it must be you, Jared. I was so frightened I couldn't even think straight. All I knew was, you had some connection with Paulette Duvaloir. What connection did you have, Jared?'

A noise on the patio outside attracted both their attentions. There were quite a number of people out there but only one — the inspector — came in through the partially open door.

'Ah, Mademoiselle Kovacks, you look much better now.' He looked at Jared then. 'We have finished here for now, but,' he added, glancing at Anya apologetically, 'we must return to ask you some questions.' Anya nodded. 'They will wait until tomorrow and in the meantime I will leave you in the good care of Monsieur Duvaloir. *Au revoir.*'

Jared watched the inspector as he left

241

the room but Anya was staring at Jared. 'He called you Monsieur Duvaloir,' she said in wonder.

When he looked at her again he smiled apologetically. 'Paulette was my sister.'

'So you're not Jared Nolan after all.'

'Jared Nolan Duvaloir. It's only my father's family who came from France. My mother is English. Nolan is her maiden name.'

Anya sank back into the cushions of the sofa. 'Why didn't you tell me?'

'I thought it best if the connection wasn't known. I assume it was Anderson who tried to brain me, so it seems I wasn't entirely successful in hiding my identity.'

'He'd seen your photograph in the locket.' She looked at him levelly. 'You came here to try and find her killer, didn't you, Jared?'

He sighed and ran his hand absently through his hair. 'I suppose so. I didn't admit that to myself but it's what it amounted to. Inspector Sandray was kind enough to let me see all the records.'

'So he knew who you were all the time, and I . . . '

He looked at her appealingly. 'I'm sorry, my darling. It couldn't be helped.'

'You just didn't trust me.'

'You were the only one I *did* trust, Anya. I couldn't trust you with the knowledge of my real identity.'

She swung her legs over the side of the sofa and got slowly to her feet. She walked across to the patio doors, staring out blindly at the pool, the garden and the row of cypress trees which hid the cliff edge from view.

'You've no idea what it's been like, Anya, to lose someone in that way. We were always a happy family. My mother and father go about their lives just as it was before, but it's different. They don't smile very much any more. It's bad enough to lose someone you love, but in that way . . . well, it's more pernicious.'

'I'm sorry, Jared,' she said in a choked voice, 'I'm really very sorry.'

'I'm satisfied now. There was never any chance of getting Paulette back, but at least he can't hurt anyone again. I just wish Cèlie had confided in me. Perhaps a few days longer and she would have done.'

'That's what Zack was afraid of. I don't think any of us need feel guilty over Cèlie, now that we know what kind of a person she was. Greed killed her in the end.'

'Once the inquests of Cèlie and Anderson are over there's nothing to keep us here any longer. The investigation is finished now. Marry me, Anya, and come back to Canada with me.'

She whirled round. For a moment she couldn't say anything and then her lips began to tremble. 'I can't, Jared, not now. Now Zack is dead I'll have to look after Penny and Jason. Helen will want them all the more now and I can't let her have them. They need me.'

He continued to look at her and

Anya couldn't bear to hold his gaze. If she did, she knew she would have to turn her back on her duty.

'*I* need you, Anya, and there's no need for you to fret about Jason and Penny. They're coming with us.'

Her eyes opened wide. 'Their father . . . '

'They are people in their own right. I don't even think of them in that way.'

'Oh, Jared, I can't let you do it! It's too much of a responsibility. They're my niece and nephew, but . . . '

'But nothing,' he interrupted mildly, holding his hands out to her. 'Stop making stupid excuses and come here and sit with me.'

Hesitantly she obeyed. Being close to him now that the shock was receding and awareness was returning once more, was a disconcerting matter. He slid his arm around her shoulder and drew her unwillingly closer.

'Penny and Jason are two nice little kids. Won't it be better for them to grow up along with our own children in a new country instead of with a rather intense spinster aunt?'

She laughed brokenly and looked up at him. 'Two children are such a commitment.'

'Commitments are what I'm after. Besides, last night you told me when this was all over you'd come with me anywhere. I'm not letting you out of that promise.'

'Circumstances have changed,' she ventured.

'In this way it's for the better. You'd have always been fretting over them. This way you don't have to. We'll all be together.

'I've got this rambling house on the banks of the St. Lawrence River — all metal and glass. It's far too big for just a housekeeper and myself. An architect friend of mine built it, you see, and he really excelled himself, although all I wanted was a small bachelor pad. It needs a family to fill it.'

'Helen won't let them go so easily.'

His face hardened. 'She's not going to have much of a choice in the matter.

At the moment she's incapable of doing anything. By the time she comes round to it we'll be married and the children will be settled with us. She'll have to fight for them under Canadian law, and I know quite a bit about that. My firm is one of the oldest in Quebec. My grandfather founded it when he came over from France.'

'My, my,' she said with an uneven laugh, 'I'm really learning about you, but not before time.'

He smiled. 'You already know all that matters. You've done a lot of moving around in your lifetime. Do you want to make this last one with me?'

She slipped her arms around his neck and allowed him to draw her closer to him, where she would always remain.

'Yes, Jared, you know I do.'

THE END